THE WAKENING HEART

Jessica Blair had been widowed for five years when she moved to a new job in the country as archivist to the Tankerton Estate — and discovered that her employer, Guy Tankerton, was as unconventional as he was good-looking. Then, working on the family papers, she stumbled on a secret about which Guy was ignorant. Its final unravelling was accomplished only when they travelled to India — and a century-old love affair at last reached its pre-ordained conclusion.

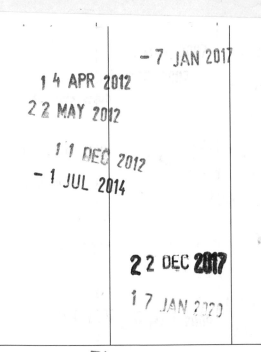

VANESSA SHAW

THE WAKENING HEART

Complete and Unabridged

LINFORD
Leicester

First published in Great Britain in 1992 by
Robert Hale Limited
London

First Linford Edition
published 2000
by arrangement with
Robert Hale Limited
London

British Library CIP Data

Shaw, Vanessa
    The wakening heart.—Large print ed.—
    Linford romance library
    1. Love stories
    2. Large type books
    I. Title
    823.9'14 [F]

    ISBN 0–7089–5651–3

Published by
F. A. Thorpe (Publishing) Ltd.
Anstey, Leicestershire

Set by Words & Graphics Ltd.
Anstey, Leicestershire
Printed and bound in Great Britain by
T. J. International Ltd., Padstow, Cornwall

1

Jessica would not have known about the job, much less applied for it, if it had not been for Mr Wilkins. It was only because of his urging that she was now approaching the severe looking receptionist at the discreet London hotel where Guy Tankerton had arranged to meet her.

'Mrs Blair?' The receptionist pretended to study a list. 'Yes, Mr Tankerton will see you in the lounge shortly. Perhaps you would care to wait there?' Her hand pointed vaguely. 'I'll let him know,' she said.

Jessica hoped that the deep grey suit with its burgundy blouse would impress him by suggesting quiet efficiency. Certainly, Guy Tankerton himself seemed well organised. A reply had come swiftly to the letter she had written offering her services.

1

'It really would be ideal for you,' Mr Wilkins had enthused. 'You are wasted here, my dear,' he had said gently, 'absolutely throwing away your qualifications.' He had gestured at the books all around him. 'A good history degree should offer you more than being an assistant, however capable, in an antiquarian bookshop.' His face folded into walnut creases as he smiled. 'Becoming the Tankerton archivist would be a step up in the world.' His pudgy fingers tapped the advertisement lightly. 'Accommodation provided without charge, away from the noise and grime of the city, absolutely idyllic.' His eyes had twinkled behind the old-fashioned steel-rimmed spectacles. 'Think how Roberta would enjoy it,' he said carefully.

That had decided her. Her daughter was five and Jessica hated the idea of her child growing up amid dull grey streets and blank-faced office blocks. She should be surrounded by green fields and trees that whispered in the wind.

It would have been all so different if Justin had not been killed, she contemplated, in a rare moment of self-pity. Roberta looked so much like her father. There were times when Jessica felt a pang of lemon-sweet memory at the sharp, inquisitive look that mirrored Justin's eager intelligence. All she had given the child, she thought sometimes, was the raven black hair, wide dark eyes and pale soft skin like silk.

She looked up as a crisp voice spoke her name.

'Mrs Blair? I'm Guy Tankerton.'

He was tall and lithe with eyes the colour of freshly opened cornflowers and his hair was like ripened wheat. His face was lean and hard, the face of a buccaneer from a story book she had loved when she was young. He was probably not yet forty, she decided, and he had the air of a hungry predator.

His dark charcoal suit fitted him to perfection and his shirt was cream silk. He wore a striped tie, school or regimental, she thought vaguely, and he

3

would have looked equally impressive in rags. A faint whiff of adventure clung to him like expensive aftershave.

He slid easily into the chair opposite her with an economy of movement that reminded her of a watchful cat. He was actually contemptuous of his surroundings, she realised with sudden amazement. He was a man who enjoyed living hard. The faded tan of his face she was sure hadn't been achieved with the help of a sunlamp or idling on a sandy beach!

'Your qualifications seem to be acceptable,' he said, 'and your employer has given you an excellent reference.' He smiled, no more than a twitch of his lips. The blue eyes were diamond hard but the voice, cultured, was unexpectedly gentle. 'Why do you want this job?'

Jessica launched into her carefully prepared little speech. She wanted to be out of London, the job she was doing did not exercise her mind enough, she felt that it was time for a change.

Her mouth was absurdly dry when she finished. It seemed suddenly very important to win his approval.

There was a faint smile on his lips when she stopped speaking. 'Now that you have got that off your chest,' he said, 'we can make some progress.' His lips pursed thoughtfully. 'You're married,' he said. It was a statement. 'Do you have husband trouble? Is that why you want to move out?' The words were spoken softly, their meaning harsh.

'I'm a widow,' Jessica said quietly. 'My husband was killed in a climbing accident.' She paused. 'The Himalayas, five years ago,' she added lamely as Guy Tankerton gave a minute frown.

She had not believed at first that Justin would not be coming back. The stammered words from an embarrassed official had meant nothing to her. It could not be true. The dream, the joy, the delight could not end just because of words.

'My apologies.' The words were

spoken without any sign of awkwardness. There was a second of silence. 'Blair,' he said slowly, 'you're Justin Blair's widow?'

'You knew him?'

Guy Tankerton shook his head. 'No,' he denied, 'but I read about it.' His eyes were full and deep. 'He was a brave man,' he said. 'Anyone else would have saved his own neck. You must be very proud of him.'

Jessica gave a sad smile. 'Somebody once said it was better to be a live coward than a dead hero,' she remarked. 'Sometimes, I find myself agreeing with that.'

Justin might not have died, she thought, if he had known that she was pregnant. His companion had fallen, broken a leg, and Justin had stayed with him, sending the other two members of the team back for help. A storm had come, delaying the rescue attempt. By the time they returned, Justin and the other climber had perished. Of the four, only Justin

6

had been married. If he had been aware that she was expecting their child, he might have acted differently. She would never know.

'You mention in your letter that you have a child.' He was frankly curious. 'It can't have been easy for you after your husband's death.' Guy Tankerton spoke firmly, not embarrassed by mentioning it as so many people had been in the past.

'A little girl. She was born seven months afterwards.' She had grown accustomed to explaining what happened after Justin died and the sentences rolled out almost without further thought. 'We were married a few weeks before Justin left. I was in my last term at university.' She could hear her own voice, wistful, recalling the past. 'That's where we met.' The future had seemed so bright, so full of promise. 'There was some life insurance and money came in from well-wishers. Enough to buy a house and furniture.' Her smile was reflective. 'Going out to work wasn't purely therapy,' she said, 'it was also something of a necessity.'

'I see.' He rubbed his hands over his face, studying her over his fingertips. 'If I offer you the post,' he said at last, 'will you be able to adapt to rural Northumberland? It's wild and craggy and rather different to life in a big city.'

'I'm sure I will be able to manage.' Jessica spoke with swift confidence, 'and I know Roberta will love it.'

Guy Tankerton frowned. 'It can be rather lonely,' he said flatly. He gave a sudden smile and Jessica saw how his lean face was transformed into friendliness. 'Let's talk about what I expect you to do,' he went on, 'and I'll try to answer any questions that you might have.'

Jessica found herself relaxing under his casual, friendly questioning. She saw him nod approvingly as she explained how she had won a scholarship to university. She had been brought up by her grandmother after her parents had been killed in a car crash when she was little.

'That's why I want to do everything I possibly can for Roberta,' Jessica said earnestly, 'it's not merely maternal feelings and instinct, I do know what it's like. I was brought up in a back-street house in an industrial suburb and I want Roberta to have everything I didn't.' She laughed. 'I didn't even know that milk came from cows until I was eight!'

Guy smiled. 'I was a little younger than that the first time I milked one,' he said. He looked at her thoughtfully. 'Technically, I suppose you're an orphan.' He raised an eyebrow. 'Is your grandmother still alive?' he asked.

Jessica shook her head. 'She died while I was at university,' she explained and did not realise how sad her smile was. 'I wanted her to see me graduate but it didn't work out that way.'

Guy nodded. 'I have a penchant for orphans,' he said lightly, 'so I guess you've got the job!'

He stood and Jessica got to her feet as well.

'Thank you,' she said nervously, 'I hope I fit the bill.'

'I'm sure you will.' His voice was confident. He held out his hand. 'I'll write and confirm.'

She took his hand to shake it and a tingle of feeling ran through her fingers like electricity at his touch.

'Till we meet again.' He spoke lightly but his eyes were serious, his fingers holding hers for long seconds.

Three weeks later, Jessica drove her small car, crammed with possessions and an excited Roberta, along the motorway which led to the north. Guy Tankerton had been very understanding although she didn't need to do very much about moving. There was a cottage on the estate for her and it was, he had assured her gravely, fully furnished down to the last spoon.

Jessica was already sharing her own house with her cousin Sarah, an actress, who had immediately offered to find another couple of tenants, two girls with whom she had been at drama school. Their combined rent added to the salary as archivist would mean that she would enjoy a comfortable income.

She gave a gasp of pleasure as her car breasted the hill and she saw Tankerton Hall, crouched in the sunlit valley, for the first time. She had left the main road twenty minutes earlier and had followed the winding lanes across the barren moorland, scarred with cragged rock and dotted with black-faced sheep.

The Hall stood proud and isolated, a band of dark green trees acting as background to its grey stone. To one side, the silvered glint of an ornamental lake, carpeted with water lily pads, basked in the sunshine. A long driveway led in a great curve to the front entrance of the Hall while masses of rhododendron bushes lined the pathways which spread out like a spider's web from the building.

Guy Tankerton walked from the Hall as she stopped in front of it. He was wearing a casual rollneck sweater of black lambswool and grey slacks which were superbly tailored to his lean, hard body. The blue eyes scanned her coolly as she got out of the car with Roberta.

'Welcome to Tankerton Hall,' he said easily. 'I thought you would like to be fairly close to the public road so I chose one of the lodge cottages as your new home.' He bent down and looked solemnly at Roberta. 'The bad news,' he said seriously, 'is that the school bus can stop there so there's no excuse for missing it even in the very worst weather.'

Jessica smiled at Roberta's tiny frown.

'I like school,' Roberta said firmly. She looked round with care. 'You have a very big garden,' she said politely.

Guy Tankerton nodded. 'It does go on a bit,' he replied gravely, 'when I was your age, I used to get lost in it.' He straightened. 'I'll come with you and lend you a hand to unload the car. I've arranged for a few supplies, bread, eggs, that sort of thing,' he announced briskly, 'all part of the service,' he added quickly as Jessica tried to thank him.

It did not take very long before the car was unloaded. The cottage was clean and sparkling and there was a cheerful log fire crackling away in the sitting room. Guy gave an approving nod as the last items were carried in.

'I hope this place suits you,' he said carefully.

'It's lovely, quite lovely,' Jessica said warmly, 'It's like a cottage in a fairy tale.'

Guy gave a swift grin. 'As long as you're not a wicked witch,' he teased, 'that's fine.' He looked at his watch. 'I'll be off and let you settle in properly,' he announced.

'Wouldn't you like a cup of tea or

something before you go?' Jessica asked quickly.

Guy looked at her. 'At this very moment,' he said thoughtfully, 'I have an irate butler tapping his fingers and wondering where I have got to.' He looked her straight in the eyes. 'I'll see you in the morning. Would ten o'clock suit?'

'That would be fine,' Jessica said. 'I wanted to take Roberta to school myself for the first day and now I can!'

'I'll show you round the house and estate tomorrow,' Guy said easily, 'and we'll talk about your job here.'

When Guy had left, Jessica sat down by the fire and gazed pensively at the yellow, bouncing flames. She had spent some time in London researching the history of Tankerton Hall and the family. She had learned that the Hall had been built only in 1860 by the first Lord Tankerton and was surrounded by an estate which had been carved out of the moorland.

Jessica had not found any mention of Guy Tankerton in the reference books she had used. He must be, she supposed, a direct descendant although he didn't seem to use the title which would have been his if that had been the case. Well, she would find out sooner rather than later — of that, she was sure!

He was waiting for her as she reached the front door the next day. 'Good morning, Mrs Blair,' he said formally, 'I hope you're raring to go on the conducted tour.' He smiled as he led the way to the library. 'We may as well start with your working area,' he said.

'I'm afraid,' Guy murmured casually as he opened the door, 'that a lot of all this is something of a cheat.' He waved airily at the shelves of books which ran along every wall of the room. 'Bought by the yard to look good.'

Jessica nodded. 'Yes,' she said cautiously, 'I was surprised to find that the Hall was built only in the middle of the last century.'

Guy Tankerton grinned. 'The proceeds of looting, Mrs Blair,' he said. 'The first and only Lord Tankerton was an officer in the East India Company's army. During the Mutiny of 1857, he acquired, by means which we need not specify too closely, a considerable amount of jewellery from the palace of an Indian prince. He promptly retired and came back to England where he bought two thousand acres of Northumbrian moorland and set about creating himself an estate and generally becoming a bigwig.'

The blue eyes were full of mischief. 'The title was awarded by Queen Victoria who was always a sucker for a handsome and gallant military man with a glint in his eye and, to be fair to my revered ancestor, he had distinguished himself during the fighting. The jewels were a little additional reward.'

Guy Tankerton laughed. 'He had only one daughter,' he said, 'and he had sent her home just before the Mutiny.

She was eighteen and something of a spitfire by all accounts. She had fallen deeply in love with a man who went off to South America or somewhere similar to seek his fortune. He never returned, died of fever according to family legend, although they wrote to each other for some years until his death. She never married and when Tankerton died, this place passed to her and eventually to a great-niece.'

'So the title died out?' Jessica said.

'The name would have vanished as well,' Guy said, 'except that Tankerton's daughter made it a condition of inheritance that the husband of the aforesaid great-niece changed his name.' His face was admiring. 'She was a pretty shrewd girl all round,' he said, 'because the other trick she pulled was to make all of this into a limited company. In addition, she invested well, putting a lot of money back into India strangely enough, tea plantations, the odd factory, that sort of thing. As a result, the estate has never been troubled by death duties.'

'I see,' said Jessica, 'and where, when and how would you like me to begin work?'

Guy Tankerton shrugged. 'When this place was built, the library was furnished by the simple expedient of going out and buying job lots of books to add to what already existed in the family. They've been added to over the years, of course, but they have never been properly catalogued. I'd like you to go through them and find out if there's anything valuable. Similarly, if there is rubbish, we might as well get rid of it. As to the family papers, there are masses of them. The same thing applies. It all needs to be listed.' He gave a chuckle. 'As there are forty thousand books or thereabouts,' he said, 'and several trunks full of papers, I suspect you may have a long job on your hands.' He smiled. 'I hope that doesn't worry you. It might take twenty years!'

Jessica grinned at him. 'It sounds like

a historian's dream,' she said, 'but I'd like to make a couple of suggestions.'

'Sure. Fire away.'

'It would make life a lot easier,' Jessica said, 'if I could put everything onto a small computer. That would only cost a few hundred pounds. I know the one I would want because I used one in my last job. We might cut the twenty years down to fifteen if we had one.'

Guy Tankerton nodded. 'That might be an argument against it,' he said as if to himself. His eyes flickered. 'Go ahead and get what you want,' he instructed. 'You'll find out about other things as we go along,' he said. 'You'll have access to everything, naturally, and I'm sure I don't have to emphasise confidentiality to you.' His voice was assured.

Jessica gave a swift nod. 'One other point,' she said slowly, 'is that every good historian likes to publish the results of research. If I did find something useful, what would be the situation if I thought likewise?'

Guy looked at her, surprise on his lean, tanned face. 'You think anybody would be interested?' he asked.

'Why not?' Jessica retorted, 'from what you've told me already, I can get quite excited at the possibilities. Lord Tankerton's daughter alone sounds as if she deserves a biography. If the material comes to light, it would be nice to write one.' She looked at him. 'What was her name?' she asked, 'you didn't mention it.'

'Didn't I?' Guy said airily, 'how remiss of me.' A tiny twitch at the corner of his mouth developed into a gentle grin. 'It was Jessica,' he said, 'Jessica Tankerton!'

'That's why I got the job, was it?' Jessica asked, straight-faced.

'Pure coincidence,' Guy Tankerton answered, 'although I don't believe in coincidence, but karma.' He gave another smile. 'That comes of spending some time in India.'

Jessica raised her eyebrows in two

perfect arcs. 'Did you go on the hippy trail?' she asked mischievously.

He shook his head. 'I told you that Jessica Tankerton invested heavily in India. There's always been a family connection which has survived until the present day.'

'Karma?' Jessica said thoughtfully, 'that's something to do with a pre-ordained fate, isn't it?'

Guy Tankerton smiled. 'More or less,' he answered, 'although it is more accurate to say that it means a chain reaction, that one small, unconsidered action can produce shattering events in the lives of others. It's rather like throwing a stone into the middle of the lake outside. The ripples spread out and destroy the bird's nest in the reeds, the stone disturbs a fish which swims straight into the mouth of a pike, that sort of thing.' His voice was very calm.

'I see,' said Jessica with a laugh, 'and you see me as a stone in a lake?'

'Hardly. But my advertisement has

already produced alterations in four people's lives. Me. Your former employer. Roberta. You. That's all I mean. Whatever happens to you from now on is a result of you answering it. Your life has changed.'

'I only hope it isn't too cataclysmic in that case,' Jessica said practically. 'I'm not someone who welcomes sudden and violent change in my circumstances. Once was enough!'

There was a sudden silence which lasted until Guy Tankerton got to his feet. 'All of the papers are stored in an office which you reach through that door over there,' he said, with a nod of his head. 'There's a telephone and all the usual gear and if there's anything else you want, let me know. I'm sure there'll be enough room even when you've installed your computer.'

There was a perfunctory knock at the door and Jessica put her hand to her mouth in astonishment as she saw the giant figure who loped, with an outrageous swagger, into the room.

He was dark-skinned with grey piercing eyes and a ferocious moustache, scarlet-turbanned, wearing white pantaloons and shirt with an embroidered waistcoat and an emerald sash. He was like something from the Arabian Nights! He spoke in a quick guttural language to Guy Tankerton who answered him in the same tongue. There was a solemn inclination of the head and the gaudy figure strutted out again without even looking at her.

Jessica gazed after him, open-mouthed.

'That,' said Guy casually, 'was the butler.'

Jessica laughed. 'Butler?' she repeated incredulously.

'His name's Wazir Khan and he is a Pathan,' Guy said seriously. 'Incredibly loyal and makes a very good butler although he does have terribly feudal ideas about his employer's property and person. Under that shirt, he was carrying a knife about a foot long so it's quite sensible not to tangle with him.'

He chuckled as Jessica gazed at him

with round eyes. 'Don't worry, Mrs Blair, you'll be perfectly safe with him around.'

The blue eyes sparkled. 'You have been honoured, actually. He's put on his finery especially and the only reason he came in was to take a look at you.' He paused. 'Pathans have eyes in the back of the head, believe me. He is no doubt describing your appearance in graphic and imaginative detail at this very moment to the rest of the household!'

Jessica shook her head with disbelief. 'Have you any other exotic staff?' she said warily.

Guy Tankerton looked at her carefully. 'As you ask, there are a few Tibetans,' he said casually, 'you'll see them and their wives in the gardens and around the house. The rest of the estate staff are mostly local, of course.'

He paused. 'A word of advice, Mrs Blair. The polite form of Tibetan greeting is to poke out the tongue. Please don't take it amiss if they do

24

so when you meet them.'

'I'll warn Roberta,' Jessica laughed, 'although I'll have to stress it's not normally polite to put out your tongue at people.' She looked at him for a long moment. 'One thing,' she said quickly, 'is that perhaps you would call me Jessica. Mrs Blair sounds too formal for words.'

The blue eyes flashed. 'You must call me Guy, in that case,' he answered, 'and thank you.' He walked casually to the door. 'Lunch is served at one o'clock and Wazir Khan is most insistent about punctuality.' He smiled. 'We've just time to look around the rest of the house before then.' The grin flickered back across his face. 'It may not surprise you to learn,' he said, 'that we will probably be eating curry!'

Jessica contemplated him with care. Guy Tankerton was more exotic than she could have imagined. A Pathan butler! Tibetans complete with wives! There was probably a herd of yaks grazing in the garden as well!

'You're looking very thoughtful!' Guy Tankerton spoke lightly.

'I was just wondering if there were any more surprises up your sleeve,' Jessica responded, 'like a few Abominable Snowmen or some yaks!'

Guy nodded. 'Not a Yeti in sight,' he assured her, his face grave, 'but there are four yaks.' He shrugged. 'The Tibs would go crazy without yak butter. They put it in their tea amongst other things.' His grin peeped across his face once more. 'It's an acquired taste, Mrs Blair, but I'm sure they'll let you try some if you're interested!'

He opened the door. 'We'll look at the exotic livestock after lunch if you wish,' he said, 'but I assure you it's harmless!'

Jessica followed him slowly. One thing was certain. Her new job promised to be a very different world to Mr Wilkins and his antiquarian books!

2

'That was utterly delicious,' Jessica said when she finished lunch. 'I have never tasted a curry quite like it!'

'I could be utterly boring on the subject,' Guy laughed, 'and launch into a history of curry which is not a dish recognised in India but rather the English idea of — ' He broke off and looked apologetic. 'There you are,' he said plaintively, 'I've started already.'

Jessica smiled at him. 'I don't mind what it's called,' she said firmly, 'it was utterly divine.'

'I'll tell Wazir Khan,' Guy said solemnly, 'and he will swagger around like a dog with two tails. As I always tell him that his meals have all the delicate flavour of aged tiger droppings, a compliment from you will make him very conceited.'

'Did it take you very long to learn

Indian?' Jessica asked after a moment.

Guy winced as if sudden pain had hit him.

'Are you all right?' Jessica was worried.

'Fine!'

'Have I said something wrong?'

Guy shook his head mournfully. 'Cue for another lecture,' he said solemnly.

Jessica looked at him curiously.

Guy raised an enquiring eyebrow. 'You're supposed to groan and make an excuse to leave the room,' he said cheerfully, 'but, as you haven't, I'll just state that there are something like four thousand different languages and dialects in India. Most educated people can speak English as well as Hindi or Urdu which are the other common languages. The last two are very similar and during the British Raj were simply known as Hindustani.'

'So you speak Urdu with Wazir Khan?'

Guy sighed. 'Sometimes we speak Pushtu but we do generally use Urdu.'

He spread out his hands apologetically. 'I told you it was complicated.'

'What about the Tibetans?'

'They speak Urdu in addition to yakspeak,' Guy said. He gave a tiny, amused smile. 'Only Tibetans and yaks can understand Tibetan,' he said, 'and Wazir Khan, like a good Pathan, is convinced that the yaks taught the people the language, hence yakspeak.'

'Where did you find the yaks?' Jessica asked curiously. The more she heard, the further removed she felt from her old life!

Guy shook his head. 'Questions, questions,' he grumbled good-naturedly. He got to his feet. 'I'll tell you as we go round the estate, otherwise we'll be sitting here all afternoon and I will spend all of the time blethering on and being boring!'

'You are not boring!' Jessica denied, 'In fact, I'm fascinated by somebody who associates with Pathans and Tibetans and yaks in the middle of the English country-side!' She put her head on one side and scrutinised him carefully. 'You didn't mention any of this at the interview!' she accused lightly.

'It didn't seem relevant,' Guy said airily, 'and it doesn't affect your work in any event.' He looked at her and Jessica saw the pleasure dancing in the blue eyes. He reached into his pocket and pulled out ignition keys. 'Let's go!'

'Can't we walk?' Jessica asked, 'it's a lovely day outside and I'm sure I'll appreciate everything so much more on foot.'

Guy smiled. 'You're a glutton for punishment,' he observed casually. 'Two thousand acres is quite a lot of ground to cover. Are you sure you are up to it? If you collapse from exhaustion half-way round, I'll have to carry you back!'

There was a heartbeat of silence before Jessica was able to respond.

'I'm heavier than I look,' she managed to answer with only the slightest tremor in her voice. 'I wouldn't wish carrying me on anyone.' She licked her lips quickly. It was absurd, the mental picture which had been conjured up by Guy's casual remark! She was acting like a moon-struck teenager!

The spring sunshine was warm on her face as they walked from the Hall. Jessica's mind was bubbling. In the years since Justin's death, she had almost forgotten what it was like to be alone with a man, particularly one who was so devastatingly attractive. She had never seriously contemplated another relationship since that black day when she had learned that she would never see her husband again.

Part of it was the complication of Roberta but, more deeply, it was because Justin had been her first and only love. It wasn't even that she still mourned him, not consciously at any rate, she told herself, but she had never been able to resist comparing anyone she met with Justin. They never measured up, never had that wonderful blend of humour and animal masculinity that had been his, never showed that quick intelligence and wry outlook which had so utterly cemented her love for him, binding the initial physical attraction into one perfect whole.

Not, she scolded herself, that Guy reminded her of Justin. They were totally different people, not even alike physically. Guy was fun and she liked him but she wouldn't think of him as anything other than her employer. She shivered involuntarily as memories jostled for attention.

'Someone walk across your grave?' Guy's voice was soft.

Jessica shook her head.

'It's chillier than I thought,' she lied swiftly, 'but I'll be fine in a moment.' She quickened her pace slightly. 'You promised to tell me how you got your yaks,' she went on, determined to change the subject.

'Zoo,' Guy said laconically, 'or rather,' he amended, 'two zoos. I started with a male from one and a female from another. Now there's five of them. It seems that if you put a male and female yak together you end up with extra yaks.'

'It's not limited to yaks,' Jessica said, without thinking.

'Quite.' Guy sounded amused. 'I did know that, now you mention it. Must have learnt about it at school.'

'I didn't mean — ' Jessica began and then stopped. Trying to explain would merely make her more confused!

'On your right,' Guy said cheerfully, 'is a path which leads to the estate offices. A brisk walk will see us there just in time for afternoon coffee!'

Jessica found the whole afternoon full of interest. Guy explained that much of the estate had been laid out by Jessica Tankerton after the death of her father. Many of the buildings dated from that time although there had been a lot of modernisation. The estate was mainly devoted to rearing sheep, pigs and cattle and the daily running was left in the hands of a farm manager.

'The main problem with the estate,' Guy said frankly as they walked back towards Jessica's cottage, 'is that the dear old lady organised it when labour was cheap. She could afford to farm some very marginal land and also allow vast tracts of it to lie idle. Not that she ground down the noses of the poor. She was very philanthropic and paid above the local wage rates.'

He grunted. 'Different story today. Even with machinery, we can't show a profit on some of the land and animals still need people to tend them. It's one reason why I've started to concentrate on specialist breeding.' Guy thrust his hands into his pockets as they walked. 'Still, we manage to get by.'

'I don't know anything about farming,' Jessica said frankly.

'Nor me, I leave it to the experts,' Guy confessed, 'but the bills sometimes seem to be heavier than the income.' He looked swiftly at his watch. 'We'd better hurry,' he said, 'your daughter will be home from school soon.'

'Would you like to come and have tea with us?' Jessica asked on a sudden impulse. 'I've got to get something for Roberta so it will be no trouble and I'm sure you could manage to drink some tea and eat some toast after all the walking about this afternoon.' She was, she realised with dawning horror, babbling like a nervous schoolgirl! Guy would get totally the wrong impression!

'I should be delighted.' He spoke with complete gravity. 'In fact, I will be able to entertain Roberta while you busy yourself burning bread and boiling water.'

They reached the cottage just as the school bus shuddered to a halt on the main road and the tiny figure of Roberta carefully clambered down. Jessica felt the familiar sensation, as if someone had tugged on a string fastened to her heart, as her daughter scampered towards her.

'So how are you settling in?' Guy called from the sitting room as Jessica busied herself in the kitchen.

'Fine,' Jessica answered, 'made easier by the fact that I didn't have to move any furniture, just personal things.' She rammed bread into the toaster. 'I know I'm going to like it here.'

'A bit different from London.' Guy came and lounged against the kitchen door as Roberta vanished towards her bedroom. 'There aren't too many bright lights around here.'

'I didn't spend many of my evenings in nightclubs,' Jessica replied carefully. She poured boiling water into the teapot and picked up the tray before moving towards the sitting room. 'Tea is served,' she said demurely.

Guy sat gingerly in an armchair as Jessica poured the tea.

'I always find I haven't the slightest idea of what to say at moments like this,' Guy said.

Jessica laughed. 'Talk about anything you care to mention.'

'Ships, sealing wax, cabbages, kings, and whether pigs have wings, perhaps?'

Guy responded. 'Name one!'

'Sealing wax,' Jessica said promptly, 'and I also know my Alice in Wonderland.'

'And Through the Looking Glass, I trust,' Guy said with a grin. 'What would you like to know about sealing wax?'

'Why is it always red?'

'It isn't,' Guy responded, 'it comes in twelve different colours — red, blue, green, orange, pink, white, black, mauve, purple — which is used only by bishops — ' He stopped for a moment and counted on his fingers. 'Grey, yellow and brown,' he finished triumphantly.

'I don't believe you,' Jessica said.

Guy looked hurt. 'It's true,' he answered.

Jessica shook her head. 'Who would use brown sealing wax, or black for that matter?' she demanded.

'Undertakers,' Guy answered swiftly, 'use black, and brown is the prerogative of the Grand Duchess of Transylvania.'

'You're absurd!' Jessica laughed.

She was suddenly acutely aware of the photograph of Justin in the silver frame on the mantelpiece. It was as if he was looking at her, ready with a teasing remark about her behaviour.

'Do you still miss him?' Guy had caught the quick flicker of her eyes as she looked towards the photograph.

'Of course.' Jessica spoke in a low voice. She turned her attention to Roberta who was wrestling with a soft-boiled egg.

'But you were only married for a few weeks?' Guy's words probed with a casual intensity.

'Why should that make any difference?' Jessica retorted swiftly. She could have kicked herself at the sharpness in her voice. Guy was treading too close to thoughts which she tried to keep buried. There had been nights, there had been times when she had wondered if her marriage would really have lasted.

'Loyalty to a dead hero?' Guy's face was blank as he spoke. 'Or better

38

to have loved and lost than never to have loved at all? At least, you have Roberta to show for your lost love.'

'I don't want to talk about it.' Jessica kept her voice calm.

'Don't misunderstand me, Jessica.' Guy's voice was swiftly gentle. 'I'm not questioning your feelings, just trying to understand them.' A note of faint bitterness trickled slowly into his words as he continued. 'Everybody has to let go sooner or later, you know. The past is in the past. Sometimes it's difficult, but life has to go on.'

'I think I've learned that particular lesson, thank you.' Jessica fought to keep her voice under control. She swallowed her tea, gulping, trying to stay calm. It wasn't fair of Guy to presume, to dig at the embers of a blaze that had been doused with such brutal rapidity on a snowy mountainside.

'I'd better go.' Guy Tankerton put down his cup with exquisite care and stood.

'It's all right.' Jessica spoke quickly and managed a smile. 'It's just that the only way I could manage at the time was not to think about it and old habits die hard.'

'I understand.' Guy was cautious.

'Do you?' Jessica asked flatly.

'I think so.' Guy was still calm. He shrugged wryly. 'I've never married,' he said slowly, 'but I did lose out once and I think I've been around enough to appreciate how you reacted, how you were able to cope.'

Jessica looked at him without speaking.

'Let me ask you another question.'

Jessica sighed. 'All right. What?'

'Why is Roberta dropping egg yolk on the carpet?'

'Oh no!' Jessica almost squeaked the words as she bent down towards her daughter. Egg was smeared all over Roberta's face.

'Let me.' Guy was already kneeling, a snow-white handkerchief in his hand, gently wiping the egg away from the tiny mouth.

'You'll ruin your handkerchief,' Jessica said.

Guy chuckled. 'My own fault. I promised to entertain her and instead I spent my time prying and poking my nose in your affairs.' His touch was deft and gentle. 'There we are,' he said, 'good as new, young lady!' He scooped up the egg on the carpet and stuffed the handkerchief back in his pocket. 'Scuffle your feet over that a couple of times,' he advised, 'and nobody will ever know!'

'At least let me wash the handkerchief for you,' Jessica pleaded, 'I feel such a fool!'

'It happens,' Guy said, 'and it wasn't Roberta's fault. She was probably fascinated by my exposition about sealing wax.' He smiled at Jessica. 'I really must go,' he said, 'I have a busy evening ahead.'

They were standing very close to one another. Without thinking, Jessica took a half pace away from him.

'I won't keep you,' she murmured.

The blue eyes were half-closed as he spoke. 'I'll see you tomorrow,' he said. His hand moved out and touched her shoulder in a brief gesture of reconciliation. 'I'm sorry if I said too much,' he muttered in a low voice before moving away to the front door.

Jessica found herself behaving like an automaton for the rest of the evening. By the time Roberta had been bathed and put to bed, Jessica was glad to sit down in the tiny kitchen and sip slowly at a cup of coffee.

She didn't know what to make of Guy Tankerton! It would be dangerous to think too much about him, she thought, watching the steam rise lazily from the brown liquid. There was a cool exterior to him and, occasionally, he let it slip. Several times, she had been acutely aware of his masculinity, the sheer magnetism of him and yet an age-old instinct had warned her not to try and get too close too quickly.

It was probably all her imagination, she decided. It was the excitement of moving, the new job, the strange surroundings and, she reasoned, the fact that she hadn't met an exciting man in five years of widowhood.

She slipped, at last, into bed and lay in the darkness, her eyes fixed on the pale ceiling. It would have been so different if Justin had not died. It was true what Guy had said about karma, about fate. Any action inevitably affected other people. Stones in lakes, ripple upon ripple. Someone she had met only once, at the reception before the climbing party left England, broke a leg and the result of that was that Roberta never knew her father. Her eyelids fluttered, becoming heavy, as she slowly began to sink into sleep.

The scream sounded perilously close. Jessica jerked into full wakefulness as the sound cut across her brain. She froze, petrified. It sounded as if someone was being attacked, a woman was being murdered. Her heart pounded and she gripped the duvet with tight, clenching fingers.

The scream came again, a long, ululating sob, filled with fear and panic. It seemed closer, almost beneath her window. Jessica knew she had to do something. She waited, counting the seconds and it sounded again, a sobbing cry which struck into her, cutting into her very bones.

She slipped out of bed and found jeans and teeshirt, putting them on, quietly, trying not to attract any attention. She dared not put on the light. Whoever was out there would see it, might turn his attention to her and Roberta. She had to do something, she told herself fiercely.

Jessica crept into the kitchen. The window faced out in the direction from which the noise had come. She peered into the darkness but she could see nothing, just the black, frightening shapes of trees and bushes, of undergrowth and an all-embracing blackness. The scream sounded yet again and the despair in it forced her into action.

There was a torch, she remembered with sudden inspiration, in the cupboard under the sink, a big, heavy, rubber-covered torch. She eased open the door and groped for it blindly, breathing a silent prayer of thanks as her fingers fastened round it. She moved, hardly daring to breathe, to the back door that led to her tiny garden, opened it as quietly and slowly as she could and stepped into the cool night.

She stood, trembling, partly-cold, partly-terrified, hoping the sound had been just imagination.

She nearly shrieked aloud as it came again, louder now that she was outside, a painful wailing that seemed to freeze her stomach. She moved forward slowly, clutching the torch, frightened to switch it on in case she attracted attention. Her mind was a blur of terror but she moved cautiously towards the dark, forbidding shapes of the rhododendron bushes.

Ten yards, twenty yards, and suddenly the bushes were all around her, their leaves rustling, seeming to reach out to claw at her. Her mouth was as dry as desert sand and she flinched as the scream sounded what seemed like only feet in front of her.

Jessica screeched as a dark shape suddenly rose from the foliage, rose in front of her and she swung the heavy torch in an arc, blindly, desperately, hearing it thud against a head, hearing the man groan as he fell away from her, and she sobbed in utter, terrified panic as arms came round from behind her, a hand grasping her breast and she saw the glint of steel slashing towards her throat and smelt the harsh mixture of scents she could not identify, on her attacker's breath.

The torch fell to the ground and there was a long moment of fear, terror scrabbling at her mind, before the knife fell away and she was spun round to face her assailant, tall, terrible in the darkness.

He moved away soundlessly. She tried to run but her legs refused to obey the summons from her brain. The man who had held her stooped down and switched on the torch with a grunt of satisfaction.

Jessica gasped as the light fell on the unconscious, dirt-streaked face of Guy Tankerton and she looked full into the unsmiling features of Wazir Khan!

3

'It was lucky that Wazir realised in time who you were,' Guy said, wincing as Jessica dabbed at his temple with cotton wool and disinfectant. 'I did tell you not to upset him.'

'How was I to know that it was you skulking around in the bushes?' Jessica demanded, trying not to sound too exasperated. She poured more disinfectant on the pad in her hand. 'It seemed for all the world as if someone was being murdered out there and I had to do something.'

Guy gave a reluctant grunt. 'I suppose I can't really blame you as you've never heard a vixen screaming before,' he admitted, 'it does sound horrible.'

'Just like a woman being attacked,' Jessica said firmly. She was fighting to keep calm, to stop her knees buckling with the relaxation of tension. The mental picture of the Pathan knife moving towards her throat was still appallingly vivid. 'You would have had to do some fast explaining,' she went on, 'if my throat had been cut.' She took a grim satisfaction in hearing Guy draw in his breath as she dabbed more antiseptic ferociously at the graze. 'Or would you have buried me somewhere on the estate and pretended I had never existed?' she demanded.

'Hardly,' Guy protested, 'and Wazir and I will speak about the matter later, I promise. I've told him not to carry that excuse for a Swiss Army knife outside the house but parting a Pathan from his blade is like trying to separate a goat from clover.' He gasped. 'That stuff stings,' he complained.

'That shows it's doing you some good,' Jessica retorted. She sneaked a look at the impassive Wazir Khan who was gazing at her attempts at first aid with a lordly contempt. He didn't show very many signs of repentance, she thought.

'Actually,' Guy said defensively, 'Wazir wouldn't really have slit your throat. But you can't blame him. He saw me being attacked and thought that he ought to wade in.'

'Which brings us,' Jessica said with sweet calmness, 'to why you were sneaking around the cottage at night, dressed in black, and looking like brigands. You're not professional Peeping Toms, are you?' She repressed a smile at Guy's embarrassment. Now that the incident was over, there was a definite pleasure in teasing him gently. She had been very frightened!

'Of course not,' Guy snapped. He sounded most indignant. 'If you must know,' he explained with an air of inconsequence, 'there's a badger sett in the woods. I was waiting for them to appear. Wazir isn't particularly into wildlife unless you can eat it and was round the other side of the copse, dreaming of nubile young maidens with big, dark eyes, I shouldn't doubt.'

Guy felt his head tentatively. 'You

50

pack a mean blow,' he grumbled, 'ever thought of going in for the world heavyweight boxing championship?'

'How kind,' Jessica murmured, 'makes me feel all that dieting is worthwhile.'

Guy blushed crimson. 'I didn't mean to imply you were fat,' he said hastily, 'overweight, that is, I meant that you have a mighty strong right arm. It was intended to be a compliment.'

'Don't trouble to explain,' Jessica said sweetly, 'and correct me if I am wrong but I don't think one is allowed to use blunt instruments in prize fighting.'

Guy covered his eyes with long fingers. 'This is not my evening,' he muttered. His hand strayed to where Jessica had hit him. 'I must look awful, all lop-sided with this bump.'

'I could hit you on the other side to even it up,' Jessica suggested gravely, 'and probably will if you continue to offer such fine compliments.'

Guy forced a grin. 'Speciality of mine,' he said. 'Anyway, the vixen was a complete surprise. I heard you come out of the cottage and start towards the trees like a herd of buffalo. Wazir must have heard you as well but he had to circle round. He didn't know who it was and arrived just in time to see you thump me with that damned torch.' He winced at the memory. 'I stood up to reassure you and then it felt like the world had fallen in on my skull. I didn't realise you were that vicious,' he joked. 'Wazir probably thought you were a poacher, reacted automatically, charged to the rescue and realised you were a woman only when he grabbed you.'

Jessica remembered the hand that had clutched her. 'Lucky for me after all that I'm not under-developed,' she said gently, and saw Guy's eyelids flicker at her remark.

Wazir Khan spoke. There was a respectful sound in the words allied with a cackling, humorous note.

'Congratulations,' Guy said dryly, 'the hired help says that you're a credit to the female race. Coming from a Pathan who resembles a tomcat in more ways than one, I think you can call yourself honoured.'

'Mummy?' Roberta's sleepy voice came from the doorway to her bedroom. 'I'm thirsty.'

'Just a moment, darling,' Jessica said automatically, 'I'll get you some orange juice from the refrigerator.' She made a final dab at the graze. 'You'll live,' she said brightly.

Wazir Khan had moved like a shadow and Jessica turned to see him kneeling down by Roberta with a glass of orange juice. Roberta's eyes were big and wide as she looked into the swarthy face of the Pathan. He spoke to her, a gentle cooing sound, and Roberta looked puzzled.

'I thought Wazir didn't speak English,' Jessica said quietly.

Guy slanted his eyes up to her and smiled. 'That doesn't mean that he doesn't understand certain words,' he returned, deadpan.

Still talking softly, Wazir Khan lifted up an unresisting Roberta in one arm and padded into the bedroom with her. Jessica heard her daughter give a tiny giggle and Wazir's voice began a low crooning.

Life is becoming ridiculous, Jessica thought to herself. My daughter is being sung a lullaby by a man who looks as if he could double for Ali Baba or one of the forty thieves. She looked at Guy helplessly. 'I don't believe all this,' she said, 'tell me I'm dreaming.'

'You're dreaming,' Guy responded helpfully. He got to his feet as Wazir Khan reappeared. 'We'll be on our way,' he announced and paused. 'It was extremely brave of you to investigate this evening,' he said quietly, 'do you mind if I say that I'm impressed?' He gave a smile which just twitched his lips and Jessica felt absurdly pleased at his approval.

She stood at the door of the cottage and watched them fade away into the darkness as they flitted, silent as ghosts, towards the Hall. It was absurd, she thought wryly, she had once believed that country life was peaceful. It was anything but that! She checked quickly that Roberta was sound asleep and then slid back into her own bed. Images of Guy jostled across her brain as she fell finally into sleep. It had all been very interesting, she thought, before her eyelids fluttered closed.

When Jessica arrived at the Hall the next morning, Guy was nowhere to be seen. She found her way to the library and looked around thoughtfully. Cataloguing the books was certainly going to be a long and laborious task.

She spent some while looking at the shelves, deciding the best way to tackle the problem. They did not seem to be arranged in any particular order and she decided that the best thing to do was to familiarise herself with what was there and provisionally jot down the various subject headings. When that was done, she could list them on the computer when it arrived.

The shelves of the bookcases ran from waist height to the ceiling of the tall room and she needed to use the wooden stepladder to reach the top. She was perched on the tiny wooden platform, peering at a long row of what appeared to be bound journals about farming when she heard the library door open. It was probably Guy or Wazir Khan, she thought, as she scribbled details in her notepad.

'No wonder Cousin Guy was so cautious when he mentioned he had got a librarian,' drawled a lazy voice. 'I always thought they were very severe ladies with pince-nez, dressed in tweeds and smelling of labradors.'

Jessica looked down, startled. The speaker was leaning negligently against the door. He was tall, with hair as black as her own, and dark eyes which had tiny gold flecks of amusement dancing in them. He was about her age, dressed casually in a faded denim jacket and jeans.

He grinned at her surprised expression

as she stared at him. 'My name is Piers Brandon,' he said and waited expectantly.

'Jessica Blair,' she introduced herself quickly. He didn't look much like Guy, even though he claimed to be a relation.

'You don't recognise the name?' he asked hopefully.

'I'm sorry,' Jessica said lightly, 'but I don't.'

Piers Brandon gave a theatrical sigh.

'Are you an actor?' she asked with sudden inspiration.

He shuddered dramatically. 'I'm mortally wounded,' he said. 'Still, it can't be helped.' He smiled and Jessica briefly saw even teeth. 'Guy said you had a history degree,' he went with blithe self assurance, 'so I suppose I can hardly expect you to be up to date on such new-fangled inventions as the camera.' He paused. 'That's a clue,' he said helpfully.

'Oh,' Jessica said, her head clearing

a little, 'you mean you're some sort of photographer?'

'That carries the unmistakable implication that I spend my time wandering along seaside promenades taking fuzzy snaps of happy holiday-makers,' Piers Brandon said sadly. The smile flitted across his lips once more. 'End of effort to impress,' he announced briskly, 'change of subject.'

Jessica stared at him. She didn't quite know what to make of Piers Brandon.

'Conversational gambit Number Two,' he began. 'Do you come here often?'

Jessica laughed. He was ridiculous. 'I work here,' she said, 'can't you tell?'

'You are far too young and pretty to be immersed in boring books,' he said firmly. 'I have already explained how lady librarians and archivists should look and therefore you are not telling the truth.' His dark eyes glowed with mischief. 'On the other hand, you seem perfectly at home on that ladder so perhaps you are really a window cleaner. In which case, where is your bucket and sponge?'

'Stop babbling,' Jessica said, trying not to laugh again.

'Only if you come down here,' Piers Brandon said coolly, 'and converse. This is a library, after all, and I demand the right to use it and to utilise the services of the custodian.'

Jessica reached the floor and looked up at him. 'Well, how can I help you, kind sir?' she enquired prettily.

Piers Brandon looked at her. 'I'd like to look at that book there.' He pointed up at the shelf where she had been. 'The third one along from the left, please.'

'You could have asked whilst I was there' Jessica replied.

'You have exceedingly good legs,' Piers Brandon said casually, 'and I get an excellent view of them when you shin up and down the steps.' The golden flecks danced in his eyes. 'I may ask you to go up and down all day.'

Jessica felt her cheeks flush.

Piers Brandon held up a warning hand before she could speak. 'Don't tell me,' he said, 'I am being impertinent but it's no sin to tell the truth and you do have very nice legs.' His face showed chagrin but his eyes were alive with humour.

'Does Guy know you're here?' Jessica managed to ask.

'Of course.' Piers sounded dignified. 'We are as Siamese twins, our thoughts are always in tune except when we disagree which is frequently.'

'Are you really Guy's cousin?' Jessica asked doubtfully. 'You talk such nonsense that I don't know whether to believe you or not. You might be a burglar for all I know,' she added.

'Do I look like a desperate criminal?' Piers Brandon's eyes were dark pools. He placed a hand on his chest. 'We are, I swear, related, although cousin might not be the right word. Very tricky.' He beamed. 'You would know about these things,' he said cheerfully, 'being used to family trees and so forth. I will tell you all about the complicated relationship if you promise to come out with me. How about tonight?'

Jessica gawped at him. 'Are you asking for a date?' she stammered.

'How delightfully old-fashioned you are in your vocabulary,' Piers drawled, 'quite 1960s style talk.' His mouth twitched into a half-smile. 'Yes,' he said abruptly.

'It's very kind of you,' Jessica said helplessly, 'but I have a five year old daughter. Someone would have to look after her.'

'That old rogue Wazir Khan will fix it,' Piers said firmly. 'One of the Tibetan women will be roped in, I shouldn't wonder.' His eyes suddenly became very firm. 'And I don't want to hear you object to one of them looking after your daughter,' he said firmly, 'it would be an honour for you and the child.'

'I wasn't going to say anything of the sort,' Jessica denied half-heartedly.

She forced a smile. 'It sounds silly, but since my husband's death, I've been out so little that Roberta isn't used to a baby-sitter, Tibetan or otherwise.'

'All the more reason for her to get used to it,' Piers replied promptly. 'I shall be here for three months and intend to take you out more than once.'

'Oh!' Jessica looked at him. 'You seem very sure of yourself,' she said, 'what happens if I refuse?'

'But you won't,' said Piers patiently, 'because I am utterly charming, frightfully good-looking, wonderful company and, to cap it all, exceptionally modest. I am also so amazingly successful that my name is a household word.' He gave an ironic smile. 'Present company excepted, you understand.'

'Do you have any faults?' Jessica asked, trying not to giggle.

Piers nodded sadly. 'I am generous beyond all measure,' he said briskly, 'something which has been remarked upon in all four corners of the globe.'

He shook his head. 'Try as I might, I cannot quarrel with my philanthropic nature.'

'You make it sound as if I have no choice in the matter.'

'Absolutely none at all,' Piers answered with a positive air. 'I will collect you at seven o'clock and we will sally forth in search of refreshment, fine wines and pleasant surroundings. I will speak to Wazir and organise an armed guard to look after your daughter. Does that sound all right to you?'

Jessica gave a helpless nod. 'Well, yes,' she said, 'but — '

'That is such an ugly word,' Piers said, 'usually prefacing a ridiculous objection to spending time in my company. The matter is settled.' He raised an eyebrow. 'I can assure you Cousin Guy won't object,' he said smoothly, 'indeed, he is always pleased to see his employees enjoying a happy social life. A recluse himself, he nonetheless gets a vicarious pleasure in knowing that others are immersed in a social whirl.'

'I would like to think about it,' Jessica said firmly. She couldn't believe that Piers Brandon was serious about Guy. It had to be his nonsensical way of speaking.

Piers inclined his head. 'Very well,' he said grandly. 'I shall appear this afternoon, confident that you will agree. In the meantime, I will arrange a baby sitter.' His hand moved in a graceful salute. 'Till later, Jessica Blair!'

Guy was already eating when Jessica went to the dining room for lunch. She was faintly relieved that there was no sign of Piers. She helped herself from the dishes that were set out on the sideboard and sat down opposite Guy. There was a large piece of white sticking plaster across the graze where she had hit him the previous night.

'I gather you have already met Piers,' he said after a few moments. 'He said he had bumped into you in the library.'

Jessica nodded. 'He said he was staying here,' she ventured.

'Yes.' Guy was elaborately casual. 'He's using one of the other cottages while he puts a book together. He prefers having his own place rather than staying in the Hall.' He put down his napkin by the side of his plate. 'He can be quite overwhelming at first meeting,' he said.

'Yes.' Jessica did not know how to continue. Guy and Piers may be cousins of a sort but she felt that there was something strange about their relationship.

'He's amusing company, I suppose.' Guy's voice was wary.

'As you said,' Jessica remarked, 'he can be a bit overwhelming.' She looked up from her plate. 'What does he actually do for a living?' she asked curiously, 'I thought he was a photographer but you say he's writing a book.'

Surprise walked across Guy's face. 'You mean you haven't heard of him?

Piers is a combat photographer,' he explained, 'you must have seen his work. If there's a war anywhere, Piers is usually in the thick of it.'

'Oh.' Jessica was nonplussed.

'Not surprisingly,' Guy went on, ignoring her tiny exclamation, 'he got his first break in Afghanistan. Some of Wazir's bhai-bund — that's kinsmen — were heavily involved in trying to throw out the Russians. Piers spent some months with them and his photographs appeared in just about every newspaper and magazine you can name. You might remember one of them, a photograph of a captured Russian pilot. It made a lot of front pages.'

'Yes,' Jessica said thoughtfully, 'I think I did see that one.' She could remember it now. A stark monochrome photograph of a fearful but still defiant prisoner surrounded by a terrifying group of Afghans, proudly clutching knives and guns.

'After that,' Guy said, 'if there

was fighting anywhere, Piers was photographing it. The book is a collection of his work with a commentary.' He gave a short, almost contemptuous laugh. 'If he stays here three months, it will be a miracle. He'll get itchy feet before long and want to be on his way to somewhere else. Piers is not one for the settled life.'

'He sounds very interesting.' Jessica winced at the inanity even as she said it.

'I'm not sure if that is actually the word I would use,' Guy said curtly. His words were sharp. 'He appeals to a certain type, I suppose.' He leaned forward across the table. 'Don't be fooled by him, Jessica. Piers can be very ruthless in going for what he wants.' He sounded embarrassed. 'He'll probably make a pass at you, sooner or later,' Guy said, 'so be careful how you respond. He doesn't mind if other people get hurt.'

Sooner or later! Jessica wondered what Guy would say if he knew that

Piers had already asked her out to dinner!

'Thank you for your advice,' she responded, a shade tartly, 'I'm a widow with a child, not some girl fresh out of the egg. I can make my own decisions.'

'I'm not trying to run your life, Jessica.'

'It sounded like it.' Jessica heard the whisper of anger in her words. She took a quick look at his face and noted the slightest tinge of colour on his cheekbones. 'I can look after myself, you know!'

'Of course. I have no right to lecture you.' Guy was absurdly formal, retreating behind a mask of disinterest. 'I may employ you,' he said with stiff dignity, 'but that doesn't mean that I own you. Spend your free time as you wish.'

'Thank you. I will.' She knew that she was being equally pompous.

'Good.' Guy spoke as if he was totally unconcerned.

'Piers said you were related,' she

observed after a few moments.

Guy nodded without speaking.

It certainly was a delicate subject, Jessica realised. Guy obviously didn't want to talk about it. Piers was ready to, though, even if the price was to have dinner with him! She wondered what the relationship really was!

'It's entirely up to you if you get involved with him,' Guy said. He was like a terrier, worrying a dead rat, unable to leave the subject alone. 'Don't blame me if you get hurt.'

'I won't.'

'Good,' Guy snapped. 'As long as your work doesn't suffer.'

'It won't!' Jessica got to her feet. She still wasn't quite sure how they had fallen out. 'I must get back to the library,' she said as sweetly as she could, 'or it will be twenty five years and not a mere twenty before I've finished!'

He gave a silent nod, not reacting to the tiny joke. The blue eyes were thoughtful, his expression careful, as she left.

And that, thought Jessica, was how to get on with your boss! Guy had been so haughty, though, she thought virtuously, lecturing her about Piers as if she had absolutely no knowledge of the world! She wasn't going to let him dictate to her!

When Piers came into the library later, her decision was made!

'Good.' He nodded briskly. 'I'll collect you at seven.'

'But what should I wear,' Jessica asked quickly, 'where are we going?'

Piers grinned. 'I shall go as I am,' he said. He paused fractionally. 'Wear something that doesn't have too many hooks or buttons,' he advised gravely, 'because it holds up the action afterwards!' He gave a tiny, mocking wink as he left her standing, speechless, looking at the closed door.

Piers Brandon arrived at precisely one minute to seven that evening. Jessica had thought carefully about what to wear. There wasn't, she realised, all that much choice. Although she had crammed quite a lot of clothes into the car when she had moved from London, most of her wardrobe was still sitting there.

In the end she chose a cotton dress, in a discreet green candystripe. Her white court shoes went well with it and she wore a plain gold necklace and gold stud earrings to complete her appearance. She had kept her makeup to a minimum and looked at her image in the mirror with satisfaction. Neat but not gaudy, she told herself, and absolutely no encouragement to wandering hands or salacious thoughts!

Piers got out of his car, an expensive-looking silver-grey sports model, and soberly opened the door for a tiny, beaming Tibetan lady. Jessica had to struggle to keep her face straight as her unusual babysitter solemnly poked out her tongue. Jessica followed her example and was rewarded by a beaming grin. Piers muttered something and the little woman dissolved into a fit of giggles.

Jessica raised enquiring eyebrows at him.

Piers smiled. 'Tibetans are happily bawdy and I made a comment about our evening together.' He seemed totally unconcerned.

'Thank you,' Jessica said shortly, 'I'm glad I'm the object of humour.' She wished she had understood what Piers had said!

'It wasn't that bad,' he explained hastily, 'sort of seaside postcard stuff but it would lose in the translation.'

They left the tiny Tibetan clucking happily at Roberta. Jessica felt a nagging annoyance. Guy and Piers could both speak these strange languages while she could only manage a few sentences in execrable French. It made her feel like an outsider. She would, she decided have to do something about it if she stayed at the Hall — which might not be for much longer if Guy really tried to run her life for her!

72

'Well,' Jessica said when they were seated in the little Italian restaurant that Piers had found, 'are you going to tell me all about your relationship to Guy or was that just a ploy?' She smiled a tiny smile. 'I don't take kindly to people who ask me out under false pretences,' she said.

He shrugged easily. 'Once we've ordered,' he said, 'I will reveal all.' He was happily at ease. 'Did I say, by the way, how utterly charming you look. Green suits you,' he went on, 'and I find your hair quite ravishingly lovely.'

'As well as my legs?' Jessica found teasing him easy.

'As well,' he confirmed gravely.

The meal was delightful. Piers chattered absurdly and Jessica enjoyed herself enormously. It had been so long since she had eaten out in a restaurant, so long since she had been with a charming man who made her laugh. It was made easier by the fact that she didn't have, didn't even want, any other sort of involvement with him. She was happily relaxed.

'You still haven't told me how you are related to Guy,' she broke in at last.

Piers looked shame-faced. 'I shall have to tell you my guilty secret,' he said. 'I come from a long line of black sheep. It's true,' he went on indignantly as she started to smile. 'We have one ancestor in common, as a matter of fact,' he explained, 'a grandfather. Guy comes from the legitimate line, I come from the other.'

Jessica studied him without speaking.

'Guy's grandfather,' Piers said, 'was married and duly produced a son who was Guy's father. He later enjoyed the company of a lady who solaced him when he was away from his wife. Hence my father. Our mutual forebear did the decent thing, however. Made sure my father was properly educated, university, all that stuff and found him a position in the family business. Running a tea plantation out in Assam as a matter of fact.'

'So your father and Guy's were half-brothers?'

'That's right. What's more, they kept in touch. Guy was older than me so we didn't see much of each other as kids but we get on well enough most of the time. We're bhai-bund, after all.' He stared at the table-cloth. 'Blood thicker than water, all that sort of thing, even though Guy thinks I'm totally irresponsible and I look upon him as a staid, unadventurous type. We're both hopelessly prejudiced in that sense. The true facts don't worry us.' He looked up at Jessica and grinned. 'The legitimate side of the family had all the money and so they paid for my education in the hope it would make an upright citizen of me. Guy, bless him, stumped up for me to go through art college when I left school and fixed things for me to go to Afghanistan.'

Bhai-bund. It was the second time that day she had heard the phrase. It meant kinsmen, she remembered, and the Tankertons seemed to take it very seriously.

'So there you are,' Piers said. 'Are you shocked?'

'No. Should I be?' Jessica asked.

Piers shrugged. 'Some people are,' he said, 'even in these enlightened days.' His dark eyes studied her carefully. 'Visit the sins of the father on the son, all that jazz.'

Jessica dabbed at her lips. 'The more I hear about the Tankerton clan,' she said, 'the more intrigued I become. Guy was telling me about Jessica Tankerton and she sounds absolutely fascinating. Guy said she was a shrewd old bird.'

Piers laughed. 'She was. The stories about her are legion. She used to trot out to India every couple of years to keep an eye on her investments. She was hardly the epitome of the retiring Victorian spinster from what I hear.'

'I hope I find out more about her,' Jessica said warmly. She looked at her watch. 'I'm sure Roberta is in the safest of hands,' she remarked, 'but

76

we should think about getting back.'

'At your service, madam,' Piers said solemnly. His eyes were tawny in the candlelight. 'We must repeat the experience.'

Piers was humming a tune softly to himself on the drive back. He brought the car to a sliding halt outside her cottage and looked at her. 'Time for bed?' he suggested softly.

'You in yours and I in mine,' Jessica said with firmness. 'It was a lovely evening, Piers, please don't spoil anything now.'

She did not hear him reply for he was out of the car, opening the door for her. She got out and they walked towards the door of the cottage. She fumbled for her key but the little Tibetan appeared and stuck out her tongue before speaking to Piers.

'Roberta is fast asleep,' he translated, 'and she is quite lovely and you are very lucky to have such a fine child.' His voice was suddenly serious. 'Thank you for a pleasant evening, Jessica.'

The eyes twinkled. 'Don't blame me for trying my luck,' he said quietly, 'you really are quite something!'

Jessica kicked off her shoes and slumped into an armchair after she had checked that Roberta was really soundly asleep. It had been a pleasant evening and Piers could be kept in check without difficulty, she thought drowsily.

She stumbled her way to her bedroom and was soon drifting into a sleep in which the images of Piers and Guy somehow seemed to float into her hazy mind before Piers drifted away entirely and she was left, dreaming of Guy Tankerton!

4

The sky was a palette of dark grey as Jessica walked to the Hall the next morning and there was a sharp breeze which tugged at her clothes and sent her hair dancing in the wind.

She wondered if Guy would visit her in the library. He would doubtless learn from Wazir Khan or the Tibetans that she had been out with Piers the night before and there was a curl of apprehension in her stomach at the thought of what he might say. Explaining that she had gone only because of his own disdainful attitude might not be the most tactful thing to say!

She wandered into her office and sat down. It would be a help, she reasoned carefully, if she knew precisely what Guy's plans were for the library. Although there were still a lot of books to look at, she was beginning to think that most of them were hardly worth cataloguing and seemed to have stayed rooted on the shelves since the day they had arrived. From her cursory inspection so far, she doubted very much if any of them were ever likely to be taken down for enjoyment.

Of course, she decided, it was possible Guy was being tactful and wouldn't come to the library. She could speak to him at lunch but he might be out. Perhaps, she thought with an obscure sense of relief, it would be best to find him and discuss the problem with him at once. It needn't be a long conversation, she thought, just enough to confirm his plans for the library and see if he would refer to the evening with Piers. If he was feeling a bit put out by it, it would give her the chance to explain. Not that Guy had any right to interfere, but he was her employer after all and that was, she reassured herself, the only reason she would mention it!

She found him in his study. The

piece of sticking plaster was much smaller. The dark, lean face was inscrutable as he looked up from his desk when she entered and sat down opposite him.

'Is this likely to take a long time?' he asked. His voice was abrupt. 'I have quite a lot of work on hand.'

Jessica explained swiftly about the books.

Guy frowned. 'I would like to realise some ready cash,' he said slowly, 'I do have a need for some.' His lips pursed in thought. 'Have you any idea what the library might fetch?'

Jessica shrugged. 'There's a lot of books there,' she began and saw him frown.

'That, Jessica,' he said, 'is a statement of the obvious. Try answering my question.'

Guy was obviously determined to be distant, even rude, unlike his usual friendly self! 'There are a lot of books there,' she repeated calmly, 'and I haven't had much chance to look at all of them.' She caught the tiniest glint of impatience in the blue eyes. 'However, I haven't found anything which would make me shriek with delight, even though I am not a complete expert.'

Guy raised his eyebrows fractionally. 'How much would they bring in?' he asked patiently.

'Frankly, most of it is only good for a second-hand stall in the local flea market.' She tried to sound cheerful. 'It would probably fetch more as waste paper. There are enough books to save a forest or two if they were recycled.'

'Very witty.' Guy toyed with the papers on his desk. 'I did just hope that there was something really valuable there. As I said some spare cash would come in very useful right now.'

He smiled for the first time as he saw the expression on her face. 'Don't look so worried,' he said, 'I'm not about to go bankrupt.' He seemed to come to a decision. 'If I tell you about it,' he said, 'it might inspire you to a great discovery.'

'I'll do anything I can to help,' Jessica said calmly, 'after all, you are my employer.'

Guy's blue eyes gleamed. 'Pity you didn't think about that before you clocked me one,' he said with a trace of humour on his face, 'I'm still seeing stars.' He leaned forward, resting his arms on the desk. 'We're back to Jessica Tankerton,' he began, 'and her legacy.' His face was thoughtful. 'She was a far-sighted old duck, very shrewd, but also philanthropic,' he said casually, 'and she decided to found an orphanage in India, in Kashmir. I'm sure you know that life is not easy there and there are a lot of parentless kids.'

His face was sombre. 'Like Topsy, the original scheme grew and grew and now there's a hospital and school as well. As you can imagine, the family has always taken an interest in it, put money in when required.' His long fingers played idly with a pencil. 'In recent years,' he said slowly, 'the need has become more pressing. There's been an influx of refugees, children driven out by warfare, kids who have stepped on landmines. They're alone, they're frightened, they need to be taught how to cope with artificial limbs and there aren't many people who give a damn about them.' There was the tiniest note of anger, of despair, in his words.

He tapped the letter on his desk. 'For years, we've been eating into the capital bit by bit. In recent times, it's really been savaged. The policy of never turning a child away has been expensive. The chickens, my dear Jessica, have come home to roost with a vengeance.' He gave a soft sigh. 'Frankly, more money is needed. Unless something is done they may have to close down completely.'

'I see.' Jessica waited for him to continue.

'It would be the easiest thing in the world,' Guy said slowly, 'to turn my back on it. Talk loudly about how the government should take responsibility, ignore the reality. Charity begins at home and all that and there are enough problems in the world anyway. Where does one begin?' he asked rhetorically.

'You could advertise for money,' Jessica said, 'lots of charities do.'

'I could,' Guy said flatly, 'but it doesn't take away from the fact that it is my responsibility. In any event, that would mean finding administrators and staff, all sorts of people and we could end up being no better off in real terms. I think I would prefer to solve the problem in my own way.'

'It's karma, isn't it?' Jessica put in suddenly. 'Your action, or lack of it, would have a disastrous effect on the lives of others who don't even know you exist.'

Guy's eyes widened. 'You did listen to my explanation the other day,' he observed, surprise in his voice. 'Added to which, my face would be blackened, as Wazir would say, if I didn't help all I can. It's a matter of honour because the complex bears my ancestor's name.

I can never forget that.'

'Jessica Tankerton set up a trust fund,' he observed, 'and that is the long-term solution. Raise enough capital so that the interest will pay the running expenses for a long time to come.'

His lips quirked into an ironic smile. 'Somewhere around half a million pounds would fit the bill nicely,' he said. Guy leaned back in his chair. 'I'm even contemplating selling part of this estate for building development,' he said, 'that's how serious I am.'

Jessica looked at him helplessly. 'Half a million pounds!' she repeated and shook her head. 'I'm sure that the library won't fetch anything like that,' she said, 'not unless there's some priceless volume tucked away somewhere but I think that's extremely unlikely.' She took a deep breath. 'To be blunt, all I've found so far is worthless Victorian rubbish.'

'You said that you weren't a complete expert,' Guy said, 'you could be wrong. There might be something there.' He gave a small grin. 'There are lots of books as you said yourself.'

Jessica returned the smile tentatively. 'There might be a few interesting items,' she admitted judiciously, 'although I obviously haven't had a chance to look at everything.'

'Well, keep looking,' Guy said, 'because I really don't want to see a row of so-called executive homes put up on land that has been the home for wildlife for the past few thousand years.'

'I do have a suggestion,' Jessica said slowly, 'which might short cut my efforts.' She stopped and looked at him.

Guy nodded for her to continue.

'If Mr Wilkins, my old boss, came up,' she suggested, 'he could look through them. He's a divvie.'

'A what?' Guy looked puzzled.

'A diviner,' Jessica explained. She smiled. 'Put him in the room blind-folded and he'll walk straight to the most valuable item there. He can tell a fake just by looking at it. He always says that he gets a tingling in his fingers which leads him to the genuine article.' She leaned forward in her chair. 'He was at a charity car boot sale once and picked out a first quarto of Hamlet in a box of old books. He said his nose led him to it the moment he walked into the room. He paid a pound for it and sold it for thousands.'

'Lucky fellow.' Guy was impassive.

'He kept 15 percent for himself and gave the rest to the charity,' Jessica said quietly. She paused. 'He really is your best bet if you want to learn quickly if there is anything of any value there.'

'It's not essential that we move with the speed of light,' Guy countered, 'the orphanage can keep going to the end of the year but they do need to know that the money will be available to carry on.' His face was contemplative. 'It's worth a try,' he said, 'perhaps you would get in touch with him and ask him to come up here. I'll pay the cost, naturally.'

'Mr Wilkins will travel at his own expense,' Jessica said serenely, 'he always does. If he finds something worthwhile, then his costs reflect in the end price.' She hesitated. 'If the library is sold in its entirety,' she observed swiftly, 'then I'm out of work.' She pushed laughter into her voice. 'Whatever happened to the twenty year plan?'

Guy raised an eyebrow. 'One week ago,' he said, 'I didn't know about this problem. Not in detail, anyway. We've had to spend so much on medical facilities alone.'

He smiled. Jessica liked that smile. 'There's a little matter of the family papers,' he said. 'Who knows? You may find a chart amongst them showing the site of buried treasure. That would be a real help!' He shook his head sadly. 'Either that, or I'll have to set up a high class brothel with the Tibetan girls as the star attractions!'

If only she did find a map! Jessica realised that she wanted to help Guy himself. The orphans were important, she didn't deny that, but she wanted to help Guy. There was a sudden, shocking thrill of revelation shooting through her. Details of her dream the previous night were suddenly sharp and clear and she knew she was blushing.

Guy chuckled at the look on her face. 'You've led a sheltered life, Jessica Blair,' he said, misunderstanding the reason for her sudden confusion. His face became non-committal. 'Did you have a pleasant evening out with Piers?' he asked with elaborate casualness.

'Yes, I did,' Jessica replied with equal unconcern. 'It was very enjoyable.' She smiled. 'Do you know that it was virtually the first time I've been out alone with a man since Justin died?'

Guy's look of enquiry was sharp.

'Oh, I hadn't become a recluse or anything,' she said quickly, 'but after Roberta was born, everything revolved around her. I didn't want to be parted from her at all. When I eventually did feel able to leave her for an evening, it was nearly always as part of a group.' She smiled again. 'Either the sympathy factor or amateur match-making or, worst of all, a convenient female to make up the numbers at a dinner party.'

'You must have met a few men who interested you.' Guy said cautiously.

'Not many men are anxious for a long-term relationship with a widow with a young baby,' Jessica answered, a thread of bitterness eating into her words, 'they prefer a short term physical affair. Most who made the offer seemed to think that they were doing me a favour!' She paused a moment. 'And it takes a good while for the memories to fade,' she said softly.

There was silence for long moments.

Guy cleared his throat. 'I'm sorry I was so self-righteous yesterday about you going out with Piers,' he ventured. 'I must have sounded an absolute prig.'

Jessica bowed her head and did not speak. If only Guy were to invite her out, there would be no hesitation on her part about agreeing!

'I'm glad you enjoyed yourself,' he said finally.

Jessica looked full into his face. 'It was very pleasant,' she murmured, 'nothing serious.' She tried a laugh. 'I'm hardly planning to elope with him!'

For a fractional moment, it was as if steel shutters had come down over Guy's blue eyes. He nodded curtly but before he spoke again, there was a tap at the door and Wazir Khan came in. He stopped when he saw Jessica and waited expectantly.

Jessica rose as Guy spoke to the Pathan. She wished she could understand what they were saying as Wazir Khan replied with a broad grin on his face.

'You'll have to excuse me, Jessica,' Guy said without emotion. 'And let me know when your Mr Wilkins is coming here!'

Which was, Jessica thought, a very cool dismissal! She could have kicked the door in frustration at the interruption. Every time she thought she was starting to get closer to Guy Tankerton, fate took a hand against her!

Jessica telephoned Mr Wilkins as soon as she got back to her office. His voice became cautious when she told him why she wanted to speak to him. He would not be able to come up to Tankerton Hall for another three weeks, he told her. That, he added, would give her a chance to at least look for something in which he might be interested. There was a faint chuckle as he explained that he was still training his new assistant.

Jessica decided to look at the trunks which contained the family papers. There were three of them, pushed tidily against one wall of the office. One looked older than the other two and she decided that she would open that first. She pushed back the lid and looked inside tentatively. It was a mass of documents, small deed boxes and dusty files. Make it another twenty years to go through all of these, she thought and reached cautiously inside to pull out the first yellowing paper.

Dust rose and she sneezed. It wasn't a map of buried treasure that she found, but a sale of a few acres to a farmer one hundred years earlier. It was, she decided wryly, going to take a long time to get the collection in order.

She began to pull out the papers with care, sorting them roughly in piles. They were mostly legal and accounting items, the small change of history as one of her tutors had called them, recording sales and acquisitions, trivia such as the price of wool when Victoria was celebrating her diamond jubilee.

The big black lacquered box, decorated with mother-of-pearl in an elaborate oriental design, was at the bottom of the trunk. Jessica puffed as she lifted it out. It was heavy and awkward to handle. She tried the lid cautiously, anticipating that it was locked, but it lifted easily and she peeped inside. There were five books with covers of burgundy-red leather and a mass of envelopes, tied together with ribbon. Locked away, free from light and dust, they looked pristine, as if they had been bought only a few days before.

Jessica squatted on her heels and opened the top book. She read for a moment with rising excitement. She picked up the bundle of envelopes, hardly daring to breathe, and with exquisite care undid the piece of pink ribbon. The name and address confirmed her suspicions and she let her breath escape in a rush. Carefully, she pulled out the letter inside the envelope with its strange stamp and scanned the page quickly. Her own name leapt out at her and she felt a darting sense of triumph. She had found Jessica Tankerton's diaries and the love letters that had been written to her so many years ago!

At lunchtime, she marched into the dining room with the air of a conqueror. She had spent the whole morning looking at the letters and had started to read Jessica Tankerton's diaries. They were made to be turned into a book, she told herself.

She blurted out the whole story to Guy as soon as he appeared for lunch. 'I'm sure it will make a good book,' she said enthusiastically, 'it might not make millions of pounds but it will earn something and we could donate the proceeds to the orphanage.' Her eyes were bright. 'It might take a year or two to write, though,' she added dismally, 'so that is not much help after all.'

'You might as well give it a go,' Guy said. He seemed pre-occupied. 'It's my problem, Jessica,' he said, 'but thank you for trying.'

'Mr Wilkins might find a gem or two yet,' Jessica said, attempting a cheerful grin, 'and solve the problem. He's coming here three weeks from today,' she added, 'that's the earliest he can manage.'

Guy gave a thin, reluctant smile. 'You probably think I'm being hopelessly sentimental,' he observed, 'but it is important to me.' He stared moodily at his plate. 'When I inherited this place,' he said, 'I didn't have a care in the world. Now it just seems to lurch from bad to worse.'

Jessica glanced at him. 'It all seems very well-run and efficient,' she commented. She wanted to reach out to him, to be a comfort. 'Things are never as bad as they seem,' she said cheerfully.

Guy looked at her. 'Is that the family motto of the Clan Blair?' he asked, a trifle sourly. He shook his head. 'I'm sorry,' he said wearily, 'but this has all come as something of a shock.'

'You're not serious about selling land for building, are you?' Jessica asked. 'Wouldn't you have to get planning permission or something.' She tried to sound efficient, knowledgeable. 'I know houses are important but so is farming.'

97

Guy shrugged. 'The estate pays its way, but that's about all,' he said gloomily. 'I don't want to turn the place into a housing estate or a theme park just to make money but the way it's going, I won't have any option.' His eyes were dark blue pools. 'I think I can put up with a few pseudo-Georgian houses for the benefit of kids who need care and love?'

It really was important to him, Jessica realised. She felt a sudden rush of tenderness. Guy Tankerton was beginning to matter to her.

When she left work in time to meet the school bus, she had the letters and the first volume of the diaries with her. Once she had finished the housework, she was going to sit down and go through them more carefully. There was also an advertisement which had caught her eye in the newspaper. Learning a language might take longer than the three weeks that was promised, but she had decided that she was going to try and master at least a little Urdu. That would really set him back on his heels!

It was late when Jessica was at last able to sit down and study the letters. She took them carefully, one by one, from their envelopes and sorted them into date order. There were twelve of them. She put the envelopes away in a drawer and settled down to read the first letter properly.

It was a weird feeling to see her own first name written at the start, as if the letter was addressed to her. She wondered what Jessica Tankerton had looked like. There was possibly a portrait of her somewhere in the Hall. Perhaps Guy even took after her in looks despite several generations having passed.

She took up the first letter. The paper was crisp to her touch. 'My Most Beloved Jessica,' it began and she started to read, immersing herself in a long-forgotten love affair, and not even the anguished cry of the lonely vixen, far off in the woods, disturbed her concentration.

5

Jessica soon settled into her working routine. She spent most of each day, feeding the new computer with information. It was tedious work but, as she worked her way steadily along the shelves, she was able to set aside a few books which she thought would be of interest to Mr Wilkins.

The Urdu language course was waiting for her one evening when she got home. There was also a postcard, brightly coloured, a picture of the Tower of London. She turned it over curiously. It was from Piers! His scrawl merely told her he was in London for a while and wanted to speak to her when he got back.

Lunchtime was something which she anticipated with a growing keenness each day. Guy chatted happily about all manner of things and she had slowly learned about his life before he had taken over the running of the estate.

His father had died when he was quite young and after university, he had gone out to India. It was then that Wazir Khan had attached himself to Guy like iron filings to a magnet.

'I must have been crazy,' Guy had laughed, 'everyone warned me about having a Pathan servant. I knew I was in trouble because after a couple of days, I caught him polishing my shoes.'

Jessica had looked enquiring.

'A Pathan cleans nobody's shoes,' Guy explained simply, 'except those of his employer. Wazir Khan had decided, I didn't argue with him and we've stayed together ever since. When Grandfather died a few years back and left me this place, Wazir Khan made it painfully obvious he was sticking with me.'

'How did you come by the Tibetans?' she asked curiously. 'Did you bring them back from India with you?'

Guy had nodded and an expression, almost of pain, crossed his face. 'They were refugees,' he said, 'teenage children when Wazir Khan and I stumbled across them. I had a hell of a job getting immigration approval for them to come here but old Jessica's foresight was handy. They became employees of the company and that made it all a bit simpler.'

It was pleasant just to be in his company, to feel the growing happiness at his presence. Guy treated her as an associate rather than an employee and Jessica found she had no doubts when he eventually asked her out for the evening.

He spoke hesitantly, as if he was fearful that she would refuse.

'Nothing elaborate,' he said apologetically, 'I was wondering if you would consider joining me in a pilgrimage to the local cinema tomorrow. We could gaze at the flickering images and, afterwards, I might be prepared to invest in a large packet of fish and chips or even a Scotch egg. What do you say?'

She didn't even ask what the film was! 'You really do make the most fabulous offer to a girl,' she said, 'and I find it impossible to resist.' She smiled at him. 'I'd love to,' she said in a low voice.

Guy looked relieved.

'Can you ask one of the Tibetan ladies to baby sit?' Jessica asked quickly.

'Of course.' Guy smiled. 'Wazir Khan will fix it. May even do it himself if it comes to the crunch.'

'I doubt that Roberta will be any trouble,' Jessica said lightly, 'she takes after her father and sleeps like the proverbial tree trunk.'

Guy laughed. 'In that case, any kids of mine will be awake all night,' he said, 'unless their mother is a heavy sleeper.'

Jessica grinned at him. 'I'm a night owl myself,' she confessed quickly.

There was a moment of silence.

'Well,' said Guy rapidly, 'I'd better go and do some work. Time is flying.' He stood. 'I'll see you later, Jessica,' he said very quietly.

The hands on her watch that afternoon seemed to be made of lead. Time crawled. Jessica could not believe that the hours could pass so slowly. It was with a sense of wakening anticipation that she finally left the library and hurried home to get ready.

When Guy arrived, the lofty figure of the Pathan peered over his shoulder. Without a word, he sidled into Roberta's bedroom and stared down at her before gliding back into the sitting room and settling in front of the television set. He gave an impatient nod as Guy translated Jessica's instructions.

'Will he be able to manage?' Jessica asked anxiously as Wazir Khan's long, bony fingers inserted a cassette into the video recorder.

'Absolutely,' Guy said cheerfully. 'Couldn't be happier, a kung-fu film to watch in which vast numbers of the ungodly are severely battered and a little girl to watch over.' He looked at Jessica. 'Don't worry,' he soothed, 'she's in safe hands.'

The cinema was old and smelt of stale tobacco smoke but Jessica felt she had never been so content. She kept sneaking a look at Guy's face, acutely conscious of his closeness. 'It's been a lovely evening,' she said as they drove home, 'and the fish and chips were excellent.'

'I did say it was nothing elaborate,' Guy rejoined, 'and I keep my word!' He paused. 'Next time, we could try something more luxurious,' he offered.

Jessica looked at him in the dim light. 'I'd like that,' she answered simply.

Wazir Khan peered from the cottage as Guy stopped the car.

'It was lovely,' Jessica repeated quickly, 'thank you, Guy,' as the Pathan strolled out to open the car door with a flourish.

'Can I tempt you in for coffee?' Jessica felt nervous.

'Next time.' The words were a promise. 'Goodnight, Jessica.'

The car door slammed as Wazir Khan settled himself in the passenger seat she had occupied and she stood and watched the firefly red lights of Guy's car vanish as he drove away.

'I don't want to cause a problem,' Jessica said carefully the next morning, 'but it's school holidays next week and Mr Wilkins will be here.' She looked at Guy's fair hair. His head was bent over the desk as he scribbled busily in the margin of a letter. 'Roberta will be at home,' Jessica explained, 'and I shall have to take time off to look after her. Either that, or I'll have to bring her to the library each day.'

Guy gave a soft grunt. 'What did you do before?' he asked.

'My cousin, who shared the house, looked after her,' Jessica said patiently. 'She's an actress so she usually had some time available during the day. When she couldn't manage it, Mr Wilkins was very understanding,' she added, 'he let me have the odd day off.'

'What makes you think I'm particularly hard-hearted?' Guy's voice was curious.

'I don't think that at all — ' Jessica began and was suddenly aware that Guy had looked up and was smiling at her.

'When I was a child,' Guy said, his voice full of memories, 'holidays were spent here. There's a lot of ground to roam in, a whole world to explore if you're tiny.' His eyes were dancing with remembered pleasure. 'Which reminds me, that ruffian Wazir Khan wants me to speak to you about Roberta. He would like to spend some time with her.'

'Really?' Jessica was cautious.

'It fits in quite neatly,' Guy said calmly. 'Like all Pathans, fierce as they may be, he has a very soft spot for children and your little beauty has won his heart. I don't think he would mind looking after her if you were busy here. Failing that, one of the Tibetan girls would be able to give a hand.'

'And how would Roberta communicate with either of them?' Jessica asked patiently. 'It's one thing to fetch a glass of juice or spend an evening babysitting and quite another to look after the child for most of the day.'

'I shouldn't think that will be much of a problem. Roberta will probably get a smattering of Urdu in no time at all and Wazir isn't a complete moron. They'll manage.'

'I wonder,' Jessica said. The taped lessons seemed to be very difficult. Perhaps she had just got out of the habit of studying. Roberta might find it easier to learn the language.

'Speaking Urdu hasn't done me any harm as far as I know,' Guy said with a straight face, 'and Piers, despite appearances, is fairly stable as well. Believe me, Jessica, Wazir will look after her like a tiger with its cubs. Give it a try,' he urged. 'They won't be far away so you can keep popping out to make sure that Roberta hasn't got up to any mischief.'

'I've always done my best,' Jessica said, 'not to smother Roberta.' It was suddenly very easy to explain to Guy. 'I've always felt that it was wrong to try and compensate for the lack of a father by being twice a mother.' She frowned. 'I believe that she should be as independent as possible.' She gazed at Guy and smiled. 'I suppose letting her out of my sight all day so that she can wander around with Tibetans and Pathans and yaks and the wild elephants which you no doubt have hidden somewhere on the estate will help her.'

Guy waved a deprecating hand. 'Absolutely no elephants,' he said with a casual laugh. His face became serious. 'Wazir Khan is not merely a butler,' he said, 'but my friend. I would trust him without hesitation with any child of mine — and he would trust me with his,' he added after a heartbeat of silence.

'You've convinced me,' Jessica agreed

pensively. She thought for a few seconds. 'If you like,' she offered, 'I'll work over this weekend. I want to try and find at least a few more books which Mr Wilkins might want to buy.' She grinned. 'Apart from anything else,' she said, 'I need to show him that I learned something during my five years as his assistant.'

'Fine.' Guy was suddenly abstracted by his paperwork. 'I'll ask Wazir Khan to come down to your cottage in the morning.'

Piers was standing idly in the library when she went back to her office. 'Good morning, Jessica,' he said brightly, 'received any good postcards lately?'

Jessica eyed him warily. 'Thank you for the view of London,' she said carefully, 'very interesting.'

'We need to talk,' Piers said. He threw out an arm. 'About us,' he added dramatically.

Jessica's mouth opened in amazement.

'It's this blasted book,' Piers said, 'my publisher wants a few cheerful photographs in it and I wondered,' Piers said cautiously, 'if you would mind if I took some photographs of you.' He fidgeted uneasily. 'Don't misunderstand me,' he carried on swiftly, 'I'm not asking you to pose nude or anything like that but I need to show my incredible versatility. I've been wandering around the last day or two taking pictures of flowers and I'd like to put you in there. Something dramatic, silhouetted by the lake, terribly arty,' he finished in a rush.

'Yes?' she prompted.

'It would have to be early,' Piers explained, 'there's a mist comes off the water at this time of year. When the sun comes above the trees it creates a super set of patterns.' He was suddenly very serious. 'They're very strong and I think you would set them off wonderfully.'

Jessica looked at him. 'Is this a try on?' she asked.

'Cross my heart,' Piers said earnestly, 'I never joke about my work. About nine o'clock in the morning would be right. I'd get everything set up beforehand and all you have to do is appear and take up the pose I tell you.'

Jessica frowned. 'I'll think about it,' she said primly. 'How long will it take?' she asked with a lingering trace of suspicion in her voice.

'Thirty minutes, I promise, no more,' Piers said promptly.

'All right,' Jessica said, 'if you're really serious about it.'

'Fine,' said Piers, relieved. He considered briefly. 'We can make it next Saturday, tomorrow week, if that's all right unless the weather forecast is absolutely foul. It is important to get the sunlight. I'll meet you at the top end of the lake at nine o'clock unless you hear otherwise.' He looked at her carefully. 'Would you mind very much wearing that dress you wore on our date?' he asked, 'the job with the fine green stripes. That would work quite well,' he said absently.

'I think I can manage all that,' Jessica said.

'Splendid!' Piers took a step towards her as the door opened.

Guy walked in.

'I thought you were working on your book, Piers?' he said. There was an undertone of steel in the question. 'Jessica does have work to do, you know.' The words were snapped out.

'Absolutely,' Piers drawled in immediate agreement, 'and I only came over to the library to ask her about a problem to which I thought she would have the answer.' Golden sparks danced in his eyes. 'A problem, Guy,' he went on, 'which influences my work on the book.' He waved a negligent hand. 'Au revoir,' he said cheerfully, 'thanks for your help, Jessica.'

'Has Piers been pestering you?' Guy grated out the sentence.

'No,' Jessica replied, picking her words with delicate precision, 'and if he should, I do know how to deal with it.'

Guy Tankerton jerked his head in an abrupt nod. 'I'll see you later, then,' he said awkwardly.

Wazir Khan announced his arrival the next day with a thunderous knocking at the door. Jessica had explained all about the arrangements to Roberta and the little girl had accepted them with complete equanimity. She squealed with delight when the Pathan lifted her high in the air and settled her down across his shoulders. Jessica felt oddly comforted at the way in which he handled her. She watched as Wazir Khan trotted away, neighing and prancing like an indignant pony, with Roberta clasping him firmly.

'You'll have to handle Mr Wilkins on your own next week,' Guy said when she arrived at the library. 'I'm sure you can do that,' he added swiftly, 'I have complete confidence in you. I have to go away for a few days,' he said. 'I leave Monday morning on the early London flight.'

'I said I would meet Mr Wilkins at

the airport on Monday so I could run you down there,' Jessica offered, 'that is, if you don't object to travelling in my little tin can of a car.'

Guy looked at her. 'You could meet me when I get back as well in that case,' he said, the tiniest hint of a challenge in his words, 'six o'clock on Friday evening.'

'I don't mind,' Jessica protested quickly. 'I could leave Roberta with Wazir Khan or bring her with me. She's usually very good if she does have to stay up.' She raised her eyes to his. 'Are you going anywhere exciting?'

Guy shook his head. 'Switzerland,' he said, 'full of yodelling cuckoo clocks made of milk chocolate,' he amplified with the swift smile that always transformed his face. 'It's business, Jessica. I'm trying to arrange a bit more support for the hospital and orphanage out in India. I'm not all that hopeful, though, because the people I am seeing are already pretty heavily committed so I expect that there will be a lot of talk and not very much progress.' He sighed. 'They do a good job but it's all the bureaucracy involved. We need a bit of action now, not in twelve months time.'

'I'll hold Mr Wilkins up for as much money as I can,' Jessica said warmly, 'I've found some books which will interest him.'

Guy smiled and Jessica felt a sudden tremor run through her at the warm expression in the gentian eyes.

'I'll leave it to you,' he said, 'you can make all the decisions.'

Guy thanked her briefly on Monday morning when they reached the terminal building and shouldered his way through to the check-in desk. Jessica was absurdly pleased when, just before he disappeared into the departure lounge, he turned and gave her a quick wave of the hand. Her own hand shot up and, with a mischievous thought, she solemnly poked out her tongue at him in the Tibetan farewell. She saw his grin and then he was swallowed up

116

by a bevy of other passengers.

'You've found one or two quite useful volumes, Jessica,' Mr Wilkins said that afternoon. His gaze swept the serried shelves. 'I suspect that there are some others here, though, all the same. If you don't mind,' he said, 'I'd like to potter about on my own.' He chuckled, wheezing like a garden gate swinging on rusty hinges. 'I may strike lucky,' he concluded.

Mr Wilkins had insisted that he would stay at a local hotel during his visit. It was, Jessica knew, his inflexible rule. He found it embarrassing, he had told her soon after she had started to work for him, to accept hospitality and then find that there was nothing that he wanted to buy when he visited big houses in the search for rare books. It was the reason, he had admitted glumly, why he still had some completely unsaleable books in the shop. He had felt so guilty that he had ended up buying things he did not want.

'Would you mind breaking your hospitality rule at least once this week?' she asked quickly. She smiled as he looked sharply at her. 'Come and have dinner with me on Wednesday,' she suggested, 'for old times sake.' She pulled a face at him. 'I'm not really a potential seller,' Jessica laughed, 'and I won't be upset if you don't buy anything.'

Mr Wilkins sniffed. 'I might bend my rules just this once, Jessica,' he said, his eyes twinkling. 'Nothing too elaborate, though,' he warned, 'no attempts to warp my judgement!'

'I promise,' Jessica smiled, 'and now I will vanish and let you sniff out the best books in the library.'

'That was a quite splendid meal, Jessica,' Mr Wilkins said happily two evenings later, 'and makes me wonder why I have remained a bachelor all my life.' He looked round with interest. 'You seem to be very comfortable here,' he observed.

Jessica nodded. 'It's a lovely cottage,'

she said, 'it's so quiet and peaceful.' She leaned her chin on her hands. 'It's good seeing you again,' she said with soft emphasis.

'My dear girl,' Mr Wilkins said patiently, 'I have enjoyed my stay and I have found a few volumes.' He sighed. 'Not that they will fetch the sort of money that Mr Tankerton needs for his orphanage.' He shook his head and smiled. 'You'll probably earn more with that book you keep telling me about.'

'It will be a long job,' Jessica said earnestly. 'I've got her diaries and letters here. You can have a look at them while I fetch the coffee.'

'I'd like that,' Mr Wilkins said, 'it always enthralls me to handle something old.'

'Her lover wasn't a prolific writer,' Jessica explained as they drank coffee, 'twelve letters over two years. I suppose the climate was pretty awful and the hard life did nothing to help. Jessica Tankerton's lover went to Canada to seek his fortune,' she explained as Mr Wilkins looked puzzled, 'and I don't think he was very successful,' she added, 'because he kept moving on.'

Mr Wilkins nodded absently as he took the letters from her and then looked at the envelopes, one by one, very carefully indeed. 'At a very rough guess,' he said in an awed voice, 'I am sitting with several hundred thousand pounds or more in my hands.'

Jessica's coffee cup dropped neatly from her swiftly lifeless fingers. She stared at the old man.

'The stamps, Jessica,' he said kindly. 'I don't know a great deal about the subject, I'm just an amateur collector myself, but I do know something about rarities.' He gave a nervous chuckle. 'One tends to browse through catalogues,' he said, 'and there's a stamp on one of these envelopes that is listed as issued, but no copy extant. I can't even begin to guess what it would fetch.'

Jessica suddenly realised that her foot

was covered with a warm liquid. The coffee squelched as she pulled off her shoe. 'Are you sure?' she managed at last.

'As sure as I can be. I must check, Jessica, just in case I've made a mistake.'

'But it's wonderful!'

'I will give you a receipt,' Mr Wilkins said practically, 'and consult with a friend of mine when I get back to London. I would suggest, if I am right, that the stamps go to auction.' He coughed. 'My terms are two percent of the selling price,' he said. 'That will be a very adequate reward for my labours.'

'Of course.' Jessica's brain whirled in a delirium of delight. There would be more than enough money for the orphanage!

'I will telephone as soon as I confirm my guess,' Mr Wilkins continued. His smile was gentle. 'I'll put these away safely,' he suggested with a low chuckle, 'while you remove the coffee from between your toes.'

She wouldn't tell Guy until she knew for certain, Jessica promptly decided. If Mr Wilkins was wrong, it would only be a terrible disappointment. If he was right, it would be the most wonderful homecoming for him.

She realised suddenly how much she had missed him during the few days that he had been away. She had found herself listening for his footsteps when she had been in the library or eating her lunch. She remembered, as if with guilt, how her heart had thudded when he had telephoned that morning to confirm his flight times. Guy had been slightly despondent, telling her that his meetings were not very promising. If the stamps did prove to be valuable, it would transform everything and be a perfect welcome when he returned!

6

Jessica took Roberta to the airport on Friday evening to meet Guy's flight and was conscious of the faintest of flutterings inside her at the thought of seeing him, a strange sensation of slight apprehension. When he walked through the barrier, his cornflower eyes searching the waiting throng, she had to make a determined effort to appear nonchalant.

'How did you get on?' she asked.

Guy shrugged. 'Much as I anticipated,' he answered, 'lots of sympathy and promises. I'm not optimistic.'

On the way back, Jessica told him about the books. It was all she could do not to blurt out the wonderful news about the stamps possibly being valuable but she hadn't heard from Mr Wilkins. It must be a surprise, she told herself firmly, she wouldn't raise his hopes. She was suddenly very much aware of how closely he was sitting next to her.

'Care to come in for a drink?' he asked as they arrived at the Hall. Guy's suggestion was tentative.

Jessica gave a tiny grimace and took a quick glance at Roberta who had fallen asleep on the back seat. 'I ought to put her to bed,' she said in resigned explanation as a faint shadow of disappointment stole across Guy's face.

'Why not come to the cottage once I've seen to Roberta?' she suggested quickly, 'I make a mean cup of instant coffee.'

Guy gave a swift nod. 'I'll get rid of this,' he said, reaching for his bag which was by his feet, 'and find out if any of the Tibs have indigestion.'

'I'm sorry?'

'It's a long story,' Guy said, grinning, 'needs at least a cup of coffee to tell it over.'

'I see.'

'All right,' Guy said, relenting, 'it's

like this. Pathans take a lugubrious pleasure in bearing bad tidings and one day, a guy comes home from a trip to be greeted by his Pathan who cheerfully informs him that everything is fine except that one of the servants has got indigestion. Caused, the Pathan explains, by over-eating. Over-eating, he adds, burnt horse-flesh. Naturally, the chap asks where it came from. From the horse that died when the stables caught fire answers the butler. Caused by a spark from the blaze that was destroying the big house. Which in turn was caused by one of the candles falling over and setting fire to the house.'

Guy paused for effect.

'But we have electricity says the distraught owner, why were candles being used? At which the Pathan bows solemnly and explains that it was one of the candles which were lit round the coffin of the guy's wife!'

Jessica kept her face straight and stayed silent.

'I can't understand it,' Guy said helplessly, 'I thought that was hilarious the first time I heard it.'

'Perhaps,' Jessica said sweetly, 'it's the way you tell it.' She began to giggle. 'Actually, I did enjoy it,' she confessed.

'So you should,' Guy said, false indignation treading his words, 'it's my one and only joke.' He opened the car door. 'I'll come down when I've dumped this,' he said. 'You'd better still be laughing when I get there,' he threatened.

There was a note on the doormat when she got home. Jessica picked it up quickly, holding a sleepy Roberta by the hand. It was from Piers, a lavish scrawl.

'Everything looks OK. See you in the morning at nine. Don't be late.'

Of course! The photographic session at the lake. She screwed the note into a ball and tossed it into the wastepaper basket in the sitting room as she passed.

She glanced at the framed photograph that was sitting on a small table. There had been a time when it had seemed that Justin would never be out of her thoughts but time had blurred the edges of the sharp memories of their few weeks together before he had gone off on the fatal climbing expedition.

If he had lived, life would have been so different, she told herself. She wouldn't have moved to London to work. Justin was going to stay on at university to read for a higher degree. He was a brilliant student, everyone had agreed on that, and he would have become a professor. They would have spent their lives in gentle towns whilst Justin rose to the top of the academic tree. They had worked it all out, excited and happy, confident of meeting the future together but everything had come to a crashing, desperate halt on a snow-covered mountain slope far away from the soft green world of England.

She tucked Roberta into bed and

wandered into the kitchen to make the coffee.

If only, she thought, she could be really sure of how she felt about Guy. Or rather, she admitted to herself ruefully, if she could be certain how he felt about her! She felt convinced that he was attracted to her, that it was not mere friendliness on his part. She wanted to feel his arms about her, needed the reassurance of his touch, but she just had to wait until he made a move in her direction.

It wasn't even that he was shy or nervous, she contemplated, as she spooned coffee into the cups, more as if he were being very cautious. There had been hints in things she had heard him say, references which made her wonder if he had been badly hurt by someone in the past.

He wasn't, she was beginning to realise, like most men she had met. He was thoughtful, too thoughtful really, and she had probably inhibited him as well. Her own words came back to her in a rush. She remembered how she had told him that not many men were prepared to take on a widow with a young child, that they were interested only in one thing. Guy probably thought she was warning him off, she decided gloomily, and would have been extra careful not to give the impression that he was only interested in her body after that remark!

She shook her head as she walked back into the sitting room and gazed once more at Justin's photograph in its silver frame. Five years. She wasn't going to rush into anything either. She was sure, as sure as she could be at this stage, that Guy was someone special but, she decided resolutely, events would just have to take their course although she was very sure that she wouldn't resist if Guy made a move towards her!

The knock on her door was soft but insistent. Jessica opened the door quietly. Her heart stopped beating for a fraction of time when she saw Guy standing there.

'I didn't want to knock too loudly,' he whispered, 'I thought Roberta would be asleep and I didn't want to wake her.'

Jessica smiled a silent acknowledgement. 'Come in,' she invited calmly, feeling her mouth dry as she spoke.

He stepped inside cautiously.

Jessica fetched the coffee.

Guy spooned sugar into his mug.

'Thank you again for a pleasant evening,' Jessica said stupidly. She didn't know what to say!

Guy cleared his throat.

'Found anything of interest in Jessica's papers?' he asked after a moment.

'I haven't had much chance to go through them,' Jessica confessed, 'time seems to shoot by in the evenings.' She ought to mention the stamps, she thought, and then decided against it. It would be too awful if it was a false hope.

He nodded absently. 'Must be plenty to keep you occupied,' he said. He shook his head. 'Sorry, that was an inane thing to say.' He supped at the coffee and put the mug down on the low table in front of him.

Silence.

'What do you — '

'What was the — '

They both tried to speak at once and stopped simultaneously.

'I'm sorry!' They spoke together.

'You first,' Guy said quickly before Jessica could open her mouth again.

Jessica shook her head. 'Nothing important,' she said, 'I just wondered how the weather was in Switzerland.'

Guy's mouth quirked. 'Very Swiss,' he said, 'highly efficient as you might expect.' He looked round the room idly and his face registered surprise.

'May I?' he said and walked across to the sideboard where Jessica had put her language course. He picked up the book and held it for a few moments before turning to look at her.

131

Jessica stood and took a pace towards him.

'Why the dickens are you trying to learn Urdu?' he asked.

Jessica was non-plussed.

'Why not?' she asked at last.

Guy's eyes were still. 'Why not, indeed?'

He put down the book. 'Making any progress?'

Jessica shook her head. 'I must be very dim,' she said quickly, 'it's hard work.'

'You need to speak it all the time,' Guy said, 'and, all of a sudden, you find it makes sense. The best method is to have a walking, talking dictionary, the sort you go to bed with.' He coughed. 'I'm sorry,' he apologised, 'I didn't mean to suggest that you should — ' He broke off in confusion.

Jessica was aware, startlingly, suddenly aware of how close he was to her. She licked her lips, a nervous darting movement of her tongue. 'There's no need to apologise,' she said, 'I'm not offended.' She tried to smile. The words sounded artificial, forced out of her.

He moved towards her.

Jessica looked up into Guy's face. His arms came round her without warning and shock stabbed through her as his lips came down onto hers. She gave a tiny mew of protest, not because she didn't want the kiss, did not realise with a sudden, engulfing emotion that she wanted nothing else, but because he was pushing her, bracing himself, his hands moving into her dark hair and she was unsteady, her feet moving backwards unwillingly. Her hands had moved automatically to push him away before she realised what she was doing and she let them fall back, passive as his lips crushed hers. She stepped back again, a half pace, and there was a clatter as she bumped into the coffee table, the sound of something falling.

Guy broke off the embrace. His eyes were hard diamonds of blue ice. He was looking past her, looking down at what had fallen. She followed his gaze and saw the face of Justin smiling up from the photograph in the silver frame.

'I'm sorry. I shouldn't have done it!' The words were a hoarse growl and Guy turned, moving swiftly, out of the room, leaving her behind him, staring with a sudden, shocking realisation that sent her blood racing through her body. She wanted Guy Tankerton!

She wanted Guy Tankerton! Jessica hardly dared believe the raging certainty that had rushed into her brain. She looked at the photograph of Justin for long moments before setting it back precisely on the coffee table.

Five years, she thought, five long years in which the idea of loving another man had only ever flitted briefly across her consciousness. She had been waiting, she realised, for someone who could instantly start the same raging fires inside her body as Justin had so casually done. She had believed that was the only route to love. Now Guy had lit the same fire, no, a more hungry blaze, she thought wildly.

It had to be reaction to the kiss, she reasoned, just a passing weakness. Seeing Guy most days, listening to him, enjoying his company, had somehow pushed him into a sharper focus and the kiss had somehow underlined his nearness.

She couldn't, she told herself, really be in love with him. The trembling in her fingers and the urgent aching inside her were liars, phantoms, which were sending messages of need which she could not fail to comprehend.

It was unbelievable. She had to get control of herself! Then the memory of the kiss, the feel of Guy's lips, the touch of his hand, the warmth and security of his arms about her, flooded in with an undeniable force and power and Jessica sat in the armchair, gazing at the photograph of Justin, and felt a long, tremulous shudder, almost of fear in its intensity, run through her body as she thought of Guy Tankerton.

Her dreams that night were full of Guy. Every time she closed her eyes, a picture of his lean, hard body came drifting across her sight.

Jessica tossed and turned, clutching at the pillow, dreaming impossible, intense dreams of Guy holding her, loving her, at last bringing her wide awake in the dark bedroom.

The cheap alarm clock that she had used ever since she was at university showed that it was still only four o'clock. Jessica lay for a few moments, staring into the dimness and finally decided to get out of bed.

She peeped into Roberta's room and made sure that her daughter was sleeping soundly before going to the shower and spending blissful minutes letting the warm water cascade over her body, watching the rivulets of foam and soap run down from her shoulders, down her stomach, her thighs, her knees, her feet.

Jessica, wrapped in her dressing

gown, sat at the kitchen table and stirred her mug of coffee idly. Guy Tankerton had kissed her and she was reacting like a schoolgirl!

It didn't mean that he cared for her. Perhaps he was a bit like Piers, just looking for an easy conquest. She dismissed the thought the moment that it came to her. She couldn't believe it, she rebuked herself angrily, because he had never made any move, never tried to touch, to insinuate, to worm his way into favour. Just the sudden, unexpected kiss, the action of a man who was shy, nervous, frightened, perhaps, of being rejected but had steeled himself to make that move and then had regretted it.

Jessica shook her head wearily. It was all so complicated and yet appallingly simple. She loved Guy Tankerton!

When Roberta had finished breakfast the next morning, Jessica set off for her rendezvous at the lake with Piers. She drove to the long expanse of water and found him busy squinting through the viewfinder of his camera.

'Beautiful timing!' he shouted by way of greeting as she walked over to him with Roberta at her side. 'What I'd like,' he explained rapidly, 'is for you to walk out on that little jetty over there and stand looking towards the Hall.' He gave a rueful smile. 'We can't use Roberta, though, so she'll have to stay behind me.'

Roberta pouted.

Jessica bent down. 'This won't take long, darling,' she explained, 'you play quietly and then we'll go and see Wazir.'

'Hurry up, Jessica,' Piers called, 'the sun's coming up and I only have about fifteen minutes before it gets too high and the effect is lost.'

Jessica reached into the car and pulled out Roberta's teddy bear. 'Here you are, poppet,' she said hastily, 'go and show Teddy the pretty flowers,' and hurried across to the jetty.

Piers worked quickly and coolly. Jessica moved as she was instructed and stood, motionless, gazing across the lake to Tankerton Hall. It was partially screened by a line of dark pine trees. Guy would probably be up by now, she thought, maybe thinking as she was thinking about the events of the previous evening. Perhaps, she thought wildly, it hadn't affected him at all, perhaps he was merely pottering about, thinking about the orphanage, wondering where he could find the money to keep it going.

She day-dreamed, imagining the look of surprise, delight and pleasure on his face when she told him about the stamps, day-dreamed that he would take her in his arms again, kiss her once more and tell her that he loved her.

The splash and the scream sounded together. Jessica whirled round to see Roberta in the water. She heard Piers swear and she was running frantically towards where she could see the bright pink of Roberta's dress a few feet from the edge. She launched herself into the lake, stumbled, and found her arms and legs meshing frantically in weeds and mud. She felt a hand on a shoulder, an arm round her waist and she was pulled upright, spitting water.

'Roberta!' she gasped.

'This lake,' Piers said calmly, 'is nowhere deeper than two feet and that's right in the middle. It's not advised to treat it like an Olympic swimming pool.' He looked down ruefully at his feet. 'That's a pair of suede shoes and a new pair of corduroy trousers up the spout,' he said.

'Mummy!' Roberta's voice was shrill, gleeful. 'Teddy went for a paddle.' Water lapped gently just above her knees.

Jessica began to giggle helplessly.

Piers steered her to the edge and then collected Roberta and a very wet teddy bear. 'The best thing you can do,' he said severely, 'is go home and have a bath.'

Jessica looked at him. 'What about you? You're wet through.'

'Only up to a few inches above the

ankles, the rest is just general dampness where you splashed lake over me,' Piers remarked. 'You are starting to shiver,' he said with sudden concern, 'in the car with Roberta, I'll drive you home.'

'Come in and dry your feet at any rate,' Jessica protested as they pulled up outside the cottage. 'Once I've cleaned up, I'll run you back to your place.'

Piers nodded. 'All right,' he said, 'while you're removing century-old water weed from your hair, I'll organise some coffee.' He looked hopeful. 'You wouldn't have a spare pair of trousers and a sweater, would you?'

'There's a tumbler-drier in the kitchen,' Jessica said, 'you can play with that while Roberta and I get clean. I do have a spare robe so you can remain decent.'

Jessica switched off the shower, wrapped Roberta in a big towel and sent her off to her bedroom to dry herself. She towelled her own hair vigorously, dried herself swiftly and slipped on her apricot dressing gown before shouting to Piers.

'Are you respectable?'

'Of course. I'm wrapped up like a chrysalis in a cocoon. Coffee's made.'

She heard the knocking at the front door of the cottage.

'I'll get it.' Piers gave a casual shout.

It was probably the postman, Jessica thought, as she went into her bedroom to find a brush.

'What the hell are you doing here?' Guy's voice was savage.

Jessica came out of her bedroom to see him standing angrily at the open doorway. His face was white, a tiny spot of colour standing harshly on each of his cheeks.

'Care for a coffee, Guy?' Piers drawled. 'We were just having one after our early morning exertions.' The words were placed with the calculated accuracy of a sniper's bullet.

'Guy!' Jessica heard the shrillness in her voice.

'I'm sorry.' His voice was harsh. Jessica could hear the snarl of breath in his throat. 'I won't intrude further,' he snapped. He turned before Jessica could say anything else and she heard the slamming of a car door and the ruthless sound of an accelerating engine.

'Dear me,' Piers said softly, 'I think Cousin Guy is a trifle upset about something. I wonder what it can be?'

7

'Why did you say that?' Jessica demanded
angrily. She fought to control her
breath. 'You made it sound as if — '

'I just like winding Guy up,' Piers
said cheerfully, 'he gets so uptight, it's
a pleasure to watch.'

The smack as Jessica's hand hit
Piers' cheek echoed throughout the
room!

'And what will he think of me
now?' she demanded, ragged indignation
spicing her words. 'I suppose that
thought never crossed your mind, it
would have spoiled your juvenile joke,'
Jessica added in a voice of ice. She
kept her eyes on Piers' face, watching
his skin redden where her fingers had
struck him.

He rubbed his cheek thoughtfully,
his tawny stare fixed on her. 'Even
Guy knows these things happen,' Piers

144

said at last. He sounded completely unconcerned.

'But it didn't happen,' Jessica countered, 'nothing happened but you deliberately implied that it had.'

Piers shrugged. 'So?' he questioned, 'Guy got the wrong impression. That's supposed to worry me?'

'And what about my reputation?' Jessica could hardly believe her ears. Piers Brandon didn't seem to care at all!

'Oh, come off it, Jessica,' he said impatiently, 'you sound like a Victorian maiden aunt. Anyway, Guy deserved it. He had the nerve to lambaste me,' he continued in his sarcastic drawl, 'just because I took you out! He was so very concerned about your welfare, it nearly brought tears to my eyes. He was worried that I might take advantage of you,' he scoffed, 'and gave me the line about you were an employee of his and not a bit on the side for my benefit.'

He gave a short, barking laugh. 'In truth, it came down to the fact that he was just waiting for an opportunity to ask you out himself. He just got miffed because I got in before him.'

'You didn't get in anywhere,' Jessica said with gritty distaste, 'nor were you likely to!'

Piers gave a dazzling smile. 'Just a question of time and technique,' he said airily, 'believe me, you would have succumbed. Anyway,' he shrugged, 'Guy didn't know that it was all very correct, did he?'

'You bastard!' Jessica spat out the words.

Piers smiled. 'That was my father,' he said coolly, 'and the main reason why Guy takes any notice of me. The dear old bhai-bund and his antiquated sense of honour.' He made a deprecating motion of his hands. 'Oh, I don't dislike him,' he said, 'in fact, I have to admire him. That's probably the trouble. He's all the things I ought to be.'

'You can go and tell him the truth about this morning,' Jessica said fiercely. 'I don't care what you feel about Guy and I don't give a damn whether he wants to get into my bed or not.' A shiver run through her as she said the words. 'I simply don't want him to think I am the sort of trollop who would get into bed with you,' she finished with increasing anger.

Piers' face was quizzical as he studied her. 'But you do give a damn, don't you?' he said softly. 'You've got your eye on him, haven't you? Well, I never!'

'I have not!' Jessica countered, her denial too fast for truth.

Piers merely laughed once more.

Jessica took a deep breath and tried to speak in even tones. 'Guy Tankerton is my employer, that's all!' Even as she said it, the image of that lean, serious face swam into her mind's eye. If she told Piers that what Guy thought of her was the most important thing in the world, he would only laugh again. 'I think the least you can do,' she said flatly, 'is to go and tell him that nothing happened between us.'

Piers guffawed. 'Not a chance! I'd rather try putting butter up a tiger's backside with a red-hot poker,' he said. 'I know Guy when he's in a tantrum. Care for another coffee?' he asked, unabashed, 'all this talking is making me thirsty.'

'You're impossible!' Jessica flared.

Piers inclined his head. 'So I've been told before,' he said.

'The best thing you can do,' Jessica said, her voice almost gravel-like as she snarled at him, 'is to get dressed and get out! You've done enough damage for one day!'

Piers looked aggrieved. 'How very curt you sound,' he observed and sighed. 'Well, Piers Brandon is known as a man who doesn't outstay his welcome in the boudoir,' he said airily, 'so I shall leave with my accustomed dignity.' He smiled. 'Perhaps, my dear Jessica, you would care to hide whilst I get dressed. Clearly, the sight of the unclothed male body would be too much for you to bear and bring on an attack of the vapours.'

His voice lost its flippancy without warning. 'You really are upset, aren't you?' he asked.

'I don't like being thought a loose woman,' Jessica said.

'How quaintly phrased!' Piers nodded slowly. 'Cousin Guy,' he murmured to himself, 'is about to sweep you into his arms when he discovers that carefree Piers is already picking the apple from the tree. That makes me a lecher and you a harlot.'

'Which is why you must explain to him!' Jessica could hear the tears in her voice.

Piers studied her carefully. 'There are times when I think Guy is a pain in the rear,' he said, 'but, deep down, I don't want to see him hurt.'

'As witnessed by your performance this morning,' Jessica said coldly.

'It wasn't until now that I fully realised that Guy was genuinely interested in you,' Piers rejoined. He paused and then said deliberately, 'and that you are interested in him.'

'All right,' Jessica admitted fiercely, 'I do find him attractive and I could fall for him. You only have to tell him nothing happened between us.'

Piers snorted with derision. 'He wouldn't believe me,' he said with flat emphasis. 'Guy doesn't trust me near a woman, any woman,' he went on, 'because I have a simple view of their purpose in this world.'

The mocking smile hovered on his lips and his eyes became tawny slits. 'I could give you a practical demonstration if you like,' he suggested, 'we don't need to have an emotional big deal to enjoy the physical pleasures of life.'

Jessica shook her head wonderingly. He was incorrigible!

'That aside,' Piers continued in calm tones, 'Guy told me that he didn't want you to be hurt, led up the garden path was the quaint way he put it, and threatened to knock off my block if I laid a finger on you.' He winced as if from a painful memory. 'He's quite capable of doing it,' he said, 'which is why I'd prefer not to beard him right now. Guy does have the habit of asking the questions after he has flattened the other party.'

'I see.'

'All I'm saying, Jessica,' Piers said patiently, 'is keep Guy at arm's length unless you are madly in love with him.'

'I'm not!' Jessica said without conviction.

'Aren't you?' Piers shot back. 'I wonder.'

He looked at her with lowered lids. 'Love isn't just a matter of leaping into bed,' he said slowly, 'not real love. Real love is gentleness and consideration, caring, wanting, an emptiness inside when the person you care for is not there, a need which is like a hunger and it gnaws inside and it creeps up on you and you realise that there is nothing you would not do for your beloved and you know that there is nothing they would not do for you.'

He shrugged. 'Sometimes, that grows out of an instant physical attraction, sometimes it's a slow awakening.' His tones were suddenly bereft, sad. 'I'm an expert on the subject,' he said, 'because I've never known it.' He walked to the door and turned. 'See you around,' he said casually.

'Thank you for the lecture,' Jessica said aloud to herself when he had gone. She looked at the photograph of Justin in its silver frame. Piers didn't know what he was talking about, she thought, had no idea. She had never had any doubt that she was in love with Justin from the very first moment they had met.

That had been an instant physical attraction, she remembered fondly. No doubt about it. It had been at a party given by another student and he had just walked over to her and her knees had turned to rubber and her stomach had churned.

She had lived for their meetings. They had been going out together for a year before they married, just before graduation. She had kept her virginity until she had become Justin's wife. He'd teased her about it, joked about old-fashioned virtue but she had wanted it to be that way. Not that there had been any real assault on her virtue. Justin was away most weekends with his climbing friends and evenings were often spent with a crowd of others when they were not studying.

Jessica decided she would have to go to the Hall herself and see Guy, explain the situation, tell him the truth about the morning. Once she had explained, Guy would have to believe her and he could always ask Piers to confirm it.

Wazir Khan shook his head gravely when she spoke Guy's name. His arms made a sweeping gesture and he shrugged his shoulders. He made a comment which Jessica did not understand but the meaning was clear enough. Guy Tankerton was not in the Hall.

Jessica thought she caught the faintest

gleam of sympathy in the dark eyes of Wazir Khan and could have cried with frustration when he merely shook his head when she asked him if he knew when Guy would return.

Perhaps she should write him a note, she thought and then decided that it would merely complicate matters even more. She needed to speak to him. The memory of the way the colour had drained from his face when he had seen her and Piers at the cottage terrified her. She must tell him the true story as soon as she could. It had to be said, not left to a note which would inevitably sound defensive.

She went to the Hall again the next day. Wazir Khan looked at her solemnly when she asked to see Guy and, without a word, showed her to the study before padding away on silent feet.

She knocked cautiously and heard Guy's curt voice. He looked at her coldly when she entered. The blue eyes were challenging points.

'Yes?' His voice was chilled, uncompromising.

'I just wanted to explain about yesterday,' Jessica began hesitantly.

'There's no need.' His voice was flat. 'You're adult. What you get up to in your own time is your affair.' His tone was dismissive.

Jessica started again. 'You don't understand — ' she said.

'I understand perfectly well.' His voice cut across her with controlled command. 'I have eyes and they work.' He ignored her attempt to break in again. 'It's nothing to do with me and I'm not interested in your sex life.' His mouth moved into a contemptuous line. 'You'll find out soon enough what Piers is really like,' he said, 'although you may be in the same mould as far as it goes.'

Jessica's eyes opened wide. How dare he compare her morals with those of Piers! She began to speak, indignant, but Guy raised his voice to drown her out.

Guy continued, his tones thin with repressed anger. 'You may as well know that Piers puts his own wishes first and be damned to others. When he tires of his little fling, he'll be off. If you get hurt, that's your problem. I don't want to know about it and I certainly don't care. If you leap into bed with the first man you meet, that is the price you pay. All I demand from you is that you do your job competently. Which, incidentally,' Guy continued without a pause, 'is why I came down and so unfortunately interrupted your session.' The words were controlled but she could hear the distaste in them.

'Wilkins called me. Those stamps are valuable. He suggested I put them into a specialist auction. There's one in a couple of months from now.'

'I don't want to talk about those,' Jessica said, 'I want to explain —

'And I don't want to hear,' Guy snapped. He paused momentarily. 'Wilkins says that the auctioneers estimate they will probably fetch better than a million pounds.' He drew a deep breath. 'I have to thank you for that,' he stated coldly. He picked up a letter from his desk. 'You'll excuse me,' he said, 'I have work to do.'

Jessica stared at him, appalled.

'Guy, please would — ' she stammered.

'Some other time, Mrs Blair.' He turned his attention back to his desk.

Jessica felt sick. It was desperately important that he knew the truth. 'There's nothing between me and Piers,' she gabbled.

'No,' he said, his voice harsh, 'there was certainly nothing but two dressing gowns between you on Saturday morning.' Guy's mouth moved as if he had tasted acid. 'Please go, before I get annoyed,' he said.

'But, please — ' she stammered.

Guy stared straight at her.

'Let's get something quite clear,' he said with an air of extreme patience. 'You want to deny that you and Piers have a relationship.' He put his hands flat on the desk. 'Fine. I hear what you say.' His eyes were cold azure chips of ice. 'That's an end to it!'

'It isn't,' Jessica cried, 'nothing happened, I swear.'

Guy stood. 'There is no point in continuing this conversation,' he said evenly, 'because I want you to understand very clearly that I am not, repeat not, interested in what you do in your own time. The fact that we went out together one evening neither gives me the right to dictate your life nor,' he paused briefly, 'should the fact that I kissed you lead you to believe you have some claim on me. Now I think you should leave before I lose my temper.'

'Won't you please listen?' Jessica blurted desperately.

'I know my cousin,' Guy said crisply.

'But — '

'Go!'

It was no use. She would have to wait until Guy had recovered his normal equable manner or at least was prepared to listen to her properly. She forced an apologetic smile and left, her stomach churning, fury fighting a desire to burst into tears!

She would have to try again the next day. That was the only answer. He couldn't continue to be hostile to her, he would have to listen sooner or later and she had to make him realise that the whole thing was a stupid mistake.

If he wasn't prepared to listen, then she would not be able to keep on working at the Hall. She'd make it very clear to him, she decided with a sudden, rushing sense of relief, that it was no use him behaving in such a way, that she wasn't prepared to be ignored.

If Guy was still intransigent the next morning, she would stand her ground and shout him down if necessary. He had to understand!

Jessica walked slowly back to the cottage, her mind in turmoil. She had not slept well the previous night, drifting off for an hour or two, dreaming absurd dreams in which Guy and Justin were scrabbling about in the snow on an icy mountain while she stood, watching, waiting, wanting one of them to triumph. Each time she had woken up before the fight had been resolved and she had sat upright in bed, remembering and wondering, hardly believing the emotions that had been surging through her in the dream.

There had been a strange, forgotten sensation, a tentative stirring of feeling deep inside her, a feeling which she forced back down into her very being, trying to ignore the half-formed, nonsensical thoughts which were jostling through her mind.

Not until the early light of dawn sneaked through the drawn curtains and she heard the birds begin to sing had she been able to bury the curious hunger that seemed to be gnawing away in the depths of her being.

Time dragged itself along the rest of the day like a cripple, passing with a slow, halting pace. Jessica decided she had to occupy herself with something useful. She would make a start on the book about Jessica Tankerton, read her way through the diaries. She had only looked at them briefly. It was an ideal way to pass the hours.

She picked a diary at random and gazed at the clear, firm handwriting. She flicked through the pages idly. It was the last journal and Jessica Tankerton had been an old woman when she wrote it so many years earlier. The words were cold and clear on the pages and Jessica started to read:

'May 24th, 1912. My 73rd Birthday and the Anniversary also of the Event. I sometimes wonder what Life would have brought to me if poor dear Charles had come back from Foreign Parts. He insisted on going, even though he knew that there was every Chance that We would not ever see each other again. I could not stand in his Way for I believed then that I Loved him and had made the Ultimate Gesture to prove it to him. It Was No Hardship for his Mere Presence set My Body on Fire. If It had been Ordained that I should become With Child as a Result of Our Endeavours, perhaps It would have dissuaded him but I doubt It.'

Jessica read the passage again, disbelieving. There was no doubt that her namesake had broken one of the strictest Victorian taboos. Jessica Tankerton had been a Fallen Woman! She was sure that Guy did not know that!

'I Consoled Myself that Charles and I, having Declared Our Love for Each Other, were married in the eyes of God even though there had been no Ceremony. And, Indeed, I counted Myself a Widow when the Awful News came. So many Years ago now but it still seems fresh in my Memory.'

Jessica felt a surge of sympathy. She could still recall with sharp precision every detail of the day when she learned that Justin had died.

'And yet when in Later Years, William entered my Life, it was as

162

if Charles was but a Shadow, the Folly of Youth. With Charles there was Demand, with William Partnership; Charles felt Impelled to Follow His Destiny, William believed We should travel Together. I think William was Mightily Shocked when I suggested, nay demanded, that he Prove His Devotion as Man and Woman have done Through The Ages. It was true that We Could Not Marry. Not Even I had that Courage but now, so many miles distant, so many years away from Each Other, perhaps I, too, should have Followed My Destiny. I can only Hope that William was Correct when he told Me that this Life is not the Sole One, that there is Reincarnation and That We Shall Meet Again in other Bodies in Future Years. It is not, I think, a Philosophy which would appeal to a Minister of the Christian Religion but it is, nonetheless, a Great Comfort. William, of course, learned it from his Oriental Mother and it no doubt appeals to him Even More as he has much Indian Thought in Him because of his Mixed Birth.'

Jessica Tankerton had found a lover who had been part Indian! Guy would be astonished to learn that as well.

She turned over the page of the diary eagerly, anxious and determined to read on.

'I have resigned Myself to Knowing that We Shall Not Meet Again in this Life. I am too Old to take again the Long and Arduous Voyage to India, that beautiful Land which Taught Me so much about Love between Man and Woman, but, even now, when I see the full Moon in the dark sky, I think of how it looked that Sultry Night when I Went to William's Room and said ' 'Mai aapsar pyar karthihu' with my eyes lowered and my hands together, declaring my love for him and submitting to him as I expected him to submit to me.'

Jessica put down the book with a soft smile. Guy's eyebrows would shoot into his golden hair when she told him about Jessica Tankerton. If she ever had the chance, she thought with a sudden pang of sadness. The old lady certainly was a determined character. She would have to go through the diaries carefully to see if she could identify the mysterious William.

It was clear that Jessica Tankerton had met him in India and she obviously had loved him, daringly for the time, and more deeply than she had loved Charles who had not returned from seeking his fortune.

Jessica read the passages about him again. There was a faint note of thankfulness, the slightest realisation that the feeling between them would have withered as time passed, something that did not apply to William. For a fleeting moment, she felt a sympathy across the years with the long-dead ancestor of Guy Tankerton. Finding love again, finding a love which somehow promised more fulfilment, more tenderness when once it had seemed that the sun would never shine again was something she was starting to understand.

And being thwarted in love, she thought to herself ruefully, was undoubtedly the most painful emotion in the world but, what bliss it would be, if it all came right!

Her dream the previous night came back to her with stark clarity. Justin and Guy, squabbling, fighting and she remembered, with a shock as if she had plunged into freezing water that she had wanted Guy to win!

8

Jessica arrived, determined to beard Guy, earlier than usual at the Hall the next morning. 'Go and find Wazir Khan, darling,' Jessica told Roberta, 'he's probably in the kitchen.'

She watched Roberta set off along the corridor towards the rear of the house. Jessica took a deep breath to steady herself. She would go to the library, start work, busy herself and then, in mid-morning at eleven o'clock, she would go to see Guy and they would talk calmly. If she went to his office immediately, he might easily get the wrong idea. She had to make sure that it didn't go wrong this time.

The hands on her watch moved so slowly that she was sure that it must be faulty. Each time she checked it they seemed hardly to have moved. Perhaps, she decided, ten o'clock was better than eleven. But she mustn't rush in, mustn't give Guy the impression that she was upset, she had to be collected, cool, reasonable until she had explained about Piers.

Ten-thirty. It was a better time than eleven, Jessica decided with a sense of grim resolution. She would wave the note from Piers in front of Guy. He had to let her explain! She took it from her handbag and walked to the library door. As she reached for the handle, it turned and Guy stood there, looking at her. The blue eyes were pools of indigo and his wheaten hair was a halo above the hawk-like face.

Jessica's heart lurched. She stared at him, pulse racing.

'I was just coming to see you — ' They spoke the words in unison and they both laughed shakily, self-conscious.

Guy inclined his head. 'You first,' he said softly.

Jessica looked at him and shook her head helplessly. 'About Saturday,' she began, 'I think — '

'I know.' He spoke calmly. 'I think I must be the biggest idiot ever born!'

'What do you mean?' Excited hope flared inside her.

Guy shook his head regretfully.

'Piers came to see me last night,' he explained slowly, 'and made me feel about four inches high.'

Relief swamped her. Piers had decided to tell Guy the truth!

'He produced,' Guy went on, 'some photographs of you by the lake.' He paused. 'They were very good photographs,' he said reflectively, 'although I have to confess I was more entranced by the subject than I was by the technique.'

Jessica could hear her heart thudding against her ribs.

'It wasn't merely that Piers made me feel an utter fool for jumping to conclusions,' Guy continued quietly, 'but that I had been so stupid as to think that you would — ' He broke off.

'It's all right,' Jessica said shakily. 'It

must have looked very compromising and after what happened on Friday evening,' she continued in a rush, 'you must have thought the worst.'

The muscles around Guy's jaw tightened. 'Yes. Friday evening,' he said awkwardly, 'I have to apologise for that as well, I think.'

'Why?' Jessica asked the question in a low tone.

Guy looked at her.

'I didn't object.' Her voice seemed to come from far away. 'In fact — ' She broke off as Wazir Khan appeared.

'Salaam, memsahib,' he greeted her solemnly. 'Chota memsahib Roberta?' he queried with a smile. The meaning was obvious.

Jessica gazed at the Pathan, in bewilderment. 'I sent her to see you when we arrived. Two hours ago,' she said in quick explanation. She heard the rattle of Guy's translation and a rapid reply from the butler.

'What's happened?' she demanded urgently.

'No need to panic.' Guy's voice was commanding. 'Wazir was out this morning, he's only just got back. Roberta is probably in the house somewhere.'

Wazir Khan whipped in with a swift sentence.

Guy nodded before the Pathan hurried away towards the kitchen. 'He's going to check if anyone saw her earlier. Don't worry, Jessica, she can't have gone far.'

A shout came from the kitchen and Guy moved down the corridor, Jessica following as Wazir Khan reappeared.

Jessica listened helplessly as the staccato, guttural exchange between the two seemed to drag on for ever. Guy was giving instructions, she could tell that. Wazir Khan's moustache seemed to grow in ferocity as he nodded his head before turning to bark orders to the two Tibetan women who were peering nervously from behind the kitchen door.

'We'll go and see if she's at

the cottage,' Guy said calmly. 'The Tibetans saw her earlier and told her that Wazir was outside. Roberta went in search of him. She's probably got tired and sat down for a rest or made her way back home. Wazir is organising the Tibetans to look round the house.'

'She could easily get lost,' Jessica said, 'the estate is huge.'

'Don't worry about that just yet,' Guy said authoritatively, 'we'll check the cottage. If she's not there and if Wazir doesn't find her, we will start looking further afield. I'll phone the estate office and ask them to keep an eye open for her.' His hand pressed Jessica's shoulder and she felt a warm surge of comfort. 'Don't worry,' he instructed firmly.

Roberta was not at the cottage.

Guy rubbed his chin thoughtfully. 'We'll take your car, if you don't mind,' he suggested easily, 'take a look round the estate roads if Wazir hasn't found her by the time we get back.'

The Pathan shook his head dolefully when they arrived back at the Hall. 'Right,' said Guy decisively, 'we'll drive around to see if we can find her.' Wazir Khan nodded swift acknowledgement as Guy spoke to him and loped away followed by four anxious Tibetan faces. Jessica waited, a sense of dread creeping through her while Guy spoke tersely to the estate manager. He slammed down the receiver and winked at her. 'All under control,' he said cheerfully, 'let's go.'

Jessica drove slowly along the winding estate roads. When they left the Hall, she had felt a cold hand clutch at her heart as she saw Wazir Khan scanning the lakeside. She knew, only too well, that it was shallow but there was always the chance of a freak accident. Guy had sensed her thoughts. 'She didn't go that way,' he said casually, 'one of the Tib gardeners was over there and she definitely didn't pass him.'

'I wish I could understand what was being said,' Jessica commented with gritted teeth, 'I feel so helpless. Why does everyone have to speak Urdu anyway?' she demanded, 'English would be quite useful under the circumstances.'

His mouth moved into a smile. 'Urdu is the language we are all at home with,' he answered gently. Guy was silent for a moment although his eyes never ceased looking from side to side for Roberta. 'Are you making any progress with it?' he asked.

Jessica did not answer immediately. Guy was only trying to make her relax, keep her from worrying too much. 'I can greet people,' she answered tersely, 'which isn't too much help at this particular moment.'

She peered at the road as it wound up a slight incline between great banks of rhododendron bushes. 'Roberta could have gone anywhere amongst that lot,' she said, 'and we'd never find her.'

'She's a very sensible child,' Guy said comfortingly. 'Takes after her mother,

I shouldn't wonder,' he added. 'If she was looking for Wazir, she would stick to the path.'

The road wound upwards, the bushes giving way to fields. 'She can't have got this far,' Jessica said desperately, 'she's only got little legs.'

'She had two hours, remember,' Guy said, 'this road goes round the fields to the estate offices and then back to the Hall. We may as well stay on it. It's misleading, Jessica,' Guy said, 'we've actually done two sides of a triangle. Roberta could easily have wandered off down one of the footpaths'

Jessica nodded. Roberta had to be close by, she couldn't have vanished and, Jessica told herself sternly, she wouldn't allow herself to be approached by strangers.

'Stop!' Guy shouted.

Jessica jammed on the brakes.

'Walking across that field,' Guy said tersely, 'one small child in a yellow dress.'

Relief flooded through Jessica. 'I'll get her,' she said.

Guy's arm came out. 'Don't rush,' he instructed, 'get out as calmly as you can.'

Jessica stared at him. 'What?'

'Do it quietly,' Guy said. His face was impassive.

He was beside her as they moved to the gate that led into the field. The determined little figure of Roberta, forty yards away, was walking steadily across to the end.

'Sixty seconds too late,' Guy muttered.

Jessica heard a snort, an animal sound of anger in the distance, as he finished speaking.

'The problem,' Guy said quietly, 'is that Roberta is sharing the field with two tons of irritated pot roast.' He pointed.

'Guy!' Jessica's eyes were wide with panic as she stared, horrified, at the bulk of the bull which was at the far corner of the field. It was peering, head lowered, suspicious of the small figure

176

in the yellow dress.

'Call Roberta.' His voice, close to her ear, was calming. 'Tell her to stand absolutely still.'

The little figure stopped and froze when Jessica shouted.

Guy sniffed. 'This is really our lucky day,' he said with a grim, humourless chuckle, 'the wind is behind us, blowing our scent straight into the nostrils of that shortsighted pile of hamburgers. Which means it's as suspicious as hell.' He studied the bull carefully. 'So far, so good,' he said, 'Annoyed, inquisitive, no more.'

'What are we going to do?' Jessica asked, controlling panic in her voice.

'Tell Roberta to take a step backwards, one pace at a time, when you tell her,' Guy instructed. His voice was utterly reassuring. He moved slowly, peeling off his jacket, putting it over his arm. He waited while Jessica relayed his instructions. 'I shall now take a stroll,' he announced calmly, 'into this excellent field until Roberta and

I meet. We will then retreat gracefully to the gate.'

'What happens if the bull charges?' Jessica asked stupidly.

'I grab Roberta and run like hell,' Guy answered. 'Don't worry. I came third in the Under Eleven Sack Race at school.' He grinned. 'Mind you, I was fifteen at the time.'

The sound of the bull snorting carried down the field. It had raised its head, catching their scent on the breeze. It moved forward cautiously a pace or two.

Guy swore softly under his breath. 'It's important Roberta doesn't turn and run,' he instructed. 'Tell her to come back one pace at a time. I will shimmy towards her like a wraith and we'll be back, safe and sound, before you can say sirloin.' He spoke casually as if discussing plans for a picnic. 'Stand by the gate and be ready to slam it shut,' he murmured, 'just in case the Sunday lunch gets angry.' He moved into the field, slowly, treading with caution. Roberta moved back a step. Guy went forward. Roberta came back closer.

The bull shook its head and snorted. Guy stood stock-still. The bull snorted again, pawed at the ground and trotted forward a few paces before halting and peering towards the intruders.

Jessica hardly dared to breathe. She felt that the sound might upset the animal. It was about fifty yards from Roberta, she thought. Guy was only a few steps from her daughter and he would be able to pick her up soon.

Guy stepped forward one pace in a gentle, flowing, almost imperceptible movement. The bull snorted, determined, and trotted forward again. The distance was suddenly down to thirty yards.

Jessica put her hand to her mouth, fighting to quell the fear that was bubbling inside her, churning her stomach. She could see the flared nostrils as the bull shook its head and its right foreleg moved, flailing at the grass. The snort came again, the horns lowered and the bull began to move forward at a surprising speed, covering the ground, charging towards Roberta.

Jessica heard a scream, realised almost at the same moment that it was her voice. She heard Guy shout and saw him start to run at a diagonal, moving away from Roberta, cutting across the bull's vision, waving his jacket. The bull swerved in its gallop, determined to counter this new threat, to challenge the creature in its domain. She ran into the field and scooped up Roberta, turned, sprinted back towards the gate and slammed it behind her, before spinning round to gaze back into the field, hugging the child tight to her.

Guy had dodged the first charge. The bull was between him and the gate and Guy was treading backwards warily, moving towards the wall which bounded the side of the field.

Jessica saw the bull's tail swish with

anger and it charged again and Guy, with the ease of a matador, swayed to one side and let it pass him. He dropped his jacket neatly on the horns and ran towards where she was standing, looking over his shoulder as the bull tossed the coat clear, trampled on it and sought its enemy once more.

Guy was only twenty feet from the gate when he whirled round to face the animal as it made another ferocious run. Jessica could hear the sound of its hooves smashing into the grass and the snuffling of its breath.

Guy stepped to one side as the bull came up to him and time went into slow motion for Jessica. There was an inevitable precision in the way in which the bull's head began to turn earlier than Guy had anticipated and a long, curved horn dragged across the white shirt and Guy was suddenly wearing a red sash, a sash which became a scarlet waistcoat as he rolled over.

The triumphant bull turned sharply,

wheeling as it came closer to the gate where she stood, and then its head went down as it prepared to charge forward and crush the shockingly still bundle that was on the ground in front of it.

'Baby in auto, memsahib, then beat it back here.' Wazir Khan's voice was a hiss as he vaulted over the gate, the long knife appearing by magic in his hand. It flashed briefly, nicking the bull's side and the bellow sounded shockingly loud as Jessica scampered to the car and bundled Roberta inside.

She ran back towards the gate, saw the bull turning to face this new persecutor, saw the white gleam of Wazir Khan's teeth and the look of pure joy that crossed his face as the bull lunged at him and he skipped away from the horns.

Wazir Khan turned and ran, drawing the bull away from where Guy still lay. Jessica knew it was up to her to get Guy out of the field, realised that Wazir Khan was deliberately giving her the opportunity. There was no need for words. The Pathan turned, the knife grazed across the bull's flank once more, goading it to fury, and Wazir Khan sprinted like the wind with the enraged bull bellowing in pursuit.

Jessica seized her moment and ran, desperation in her heart to where Guy lay. There was no time to think, she had to get him to safety. 'Darling, darling, please don't die,' she muttered as she pushed her arms under his body, feeling the damp stickiness of the blood and she dragged him, panting, sobbing, towards the gate.

Twenty feet, fifteen, ten, five and she was through the gate, on the road, kneeling by him, trying to staunch the blood from the long thin gash in his side. She pulled off her blouse, crushed it as tight as she could and pressed it to the cut, a new tremor gripping her as it immediately began to turn crimson.

'OK, memsahib.' Wazir Khan was beside her. He pointed to the car. 'Teffylone, doctor sahib,' he instructed, dark fingers deftly refolding her suddenly, shockingly, bloody blouse into a neat pad. 'Jaldhi, memsahib,' he urged and when she hesitated, added in a shocking American accent, 'shift it, sister!'

Jessica screeched to a halt in front of the Hall. Roberta was tearful, moving into shock, and one of the Tibetan women clucked her tongue, grabbing the child, soothing her as Jessica ran to the telephone.

Her fingers stabbed the buttons for the emergency service and she found herself speaking to a calm controller while the remaining Tibetans gathered round her solemnly. Jessica tried desperately to remember her few words of Urdu. She had played three taped lessons and her mind was horribly blank.

She pointed desperately up towards the field and made a snorting noise, lowered her head and shook it. The Tibetans looked blank. 'Sahib Guy,' she said firmly, 'jaldhi, jaldhi, Wazir Khan.' Three heads bobbed in sudden, swift comprehension, there was the clatter of urgent speech and the two men turned around and hurried away.

Jessica wondered how long the ambulance would take. Guy had looked awful and she felt a desperate need to be close to him, by his side, watching, hoping, giving him strength but she had to wait for the ambulance, wait for it to arrive at the Hall and show the way to the field.

Roberta had been miraculously whisked away and one of the Tibetan women made a smiling gesture, hurrying up to Jessica with a dark grey sweater. Jessica looked at it blankly and suddenly realised that she was wearing only a bra and skirt. Her blouse, she remembered, with a sudden, wrenching feeling, was still soaking up Guy's blood.

She pulled the sweater hastily over her head, realised it must be Guy's because of its size, and the warm animal feel of the wool seemed to bring him close to her. Jessica moved towards the front door of the Hall.

Roberta would be comforted by the distressed Tibetan girls, Jessica thought hurriedly, as she got into the car and started the engine, hearing the distant sound of the siren as the ambulance approached.

Guy's eyelids fluttered open briefly as he was loaded into the ambulance. His smile was weak as his eyes focussed on Jessica. 'I should have mentioned I had twenty yards start in the sack race,' he muttered before his eyes closed again.

Wazir Khan stepped forward and got into the ambulance as the stretcher was loaded. Jessica hastily ushered the two Tibetans into her car and followed the ambulance as it picked its way down the track. As they passed the Hall, Piers stepped forward. The Tibetans climbed out and Piers got in beside her. 'Follow that vehicle,' he said languidly.

'I was going to,' Jessica snarled, 'what do you want?'

'Guy and I have the same blood group,' Piers answered, 'not too common, actually, comes of being related, I dare say.' He hunched in the seat. 'Heard the siren,' he explained briefly, 'drifted across to the Hall, got the garbled gist of the story from one of the Tib wives. How bad is he?'

Jessica fought back sudden, biting salt tears. 'He was gored,' she said wretchedly, 'he seems to have lost a lot of blood but he was conscious when they put him on the stretcher.'

'Tough as old boots is Guy,' Piers said laconically. He stared through the windscreen as the ambulance turned on to the public road. 'Cottage Hospital in Glanby,' he said with satisfaction, 'so he can't be too bad.'

Jessica tried not to sniff. 'They might not want to risk taking him any further,' she said miserably.

'Optimism is your strength,' Piers said cuttingly, 'shines out of you like a big light. He'll be fine. Be skipping about like a spring lamb inside a fortnight, I'll be bound.'

It was a long wait at the small

hospital. Piers was hustled away as soon as he had spoken to the doctor. Wazir Khan was nowhere to be seen. Jessica sat alone, ignoring the curious looks of passing nurses. Guy had to be all right, he would survive. She repeated the thought to herself, over and over, a litany against disaster. Guy would pull through.

Piers returned. 'One pint of Tankerton best,' he announced, 'bound to sort him out, considering the source,' he said casually.

The doctor appeared at last.

Jessica got to her feet slowly, fearing what he would say.

'You can both go and see him now.' The accent was Scottish, calm, oozing competence. 'He's conscious and he'll mend but he'll be in here for a few days yet. You won't be able to stay long because I've given him a sedative. He'll be dropping off into a good sleep, nature's way of healing, you'll understand,' he said pedantically.

'I want to stay with him,' Jessica said hurriedly.

The doctor sighed. 'It's like Piccadilly Circus in there already,' he said resignedly, 'that damned bandit with a knife refused to leave all the way through my cleaning up so I won't even try to get him out of the room.' He grimaced and looked at her. 'Perhaps you can control him. The patient will get his rest, all the same, I've seen to that.'

Jessica just shook her head, trying to find words, when she saw Guy in the hospital bed. 'Thank you for saving Roberta,' she finally managed.

Guy's smile flitted wearily across his face. 'You returned the favour,' he managed and winced. He looked at Piers. 'Thanks for the loan of the blood,' he said, 'hope you don't need it back in a hurry.'

Piers shrugged. 'Only if I offer dinner to a lady vampire bat,' he answered shortly. 'Lucky I was around actually,' he said, 'if you'd got yourself into

189

trouble tomorrow, you'd have been forced to make do with inferior stuff.'

Guy's face was questioning. 'Off on your travels again?' he asked with a thin smile.

'That's right. Middle East next stop. Couldn't refuse, really. Gets boring around here and I refuse to play gooseberry.' The words dropped like stones into a still pool.

Piers put his head close to Guy's face. 'Don't mess it up,' he said in a fierce whisper. He turned to look at Jessica. 'That goes for you as well,' he instructed, 'and send me an invitation to the wedding. I probably won't be able to manage it, but it's nice to be asked.'

There was silence in the room when Piers had left. On an impulse, Jessica reached out and took Guy's hand. His eyes had closed again and she leaned forward as his lips moved.

'I don't want to go to sleep,' he murmured drowsily, 'lots to talk about, must be this damned drug.' The words came out as if plucked from him as single hairs. 'Did you mean what you said when I was shamming dead?' His head lolled to one side and Jessica sat, gazing joyfully, at the man she loved!

9

Jessica, luxuriating in the warm, scented water, lay in the bath and tried to ignore the flutter of anticipation and apprehension in her stomach. Guy had been discharged from the hospital after ten days, bruised, bandaged, but cheerful. Jessica had the suspicion that the staff had released him as soon as they dared because it was the easiest way to remove Wazir Khan from the premises! The Pathan had simply refused to leave.

Jessica grinned at the memory of the fierce staff nurse whose attempts to force Wazir to depart had been met with a seraphic smile and a burst of politely murmured Pushtu. When that had proved insufficient, Wazir had started to clean his nails with the point of his very sharp knife.

The staff nurse had retreated,

muttering about calling the police, offensive weapons, unofficial visitors and Jessica had spent twenty minutes calming her down. Guy had nearly burst his stitches with laughter. The gently spoken phrase, accompanied by the charming smile, translated into an unflattering suggestion. 'Go and make babies with a blind water buffalo,' Wazir had said.

Guy's easy charm had finally won the day and Wazir Khan had stayed, leaving Guy only when Jessica visited him. They had talked a lot, the visits lasting longer in the private room as Guy got stronger.

Jessica studied her fingernails critically. They could do with the gentlest of manicures and she would use a clear polish on them or perhaps a very pale pink one. She would give her toenails the same treatment, she decided, preparing herself for the evening ahead with the greatest care.

It had taken another two weeks since Guy had left the hospital for him to be really comfortable. The bruises had faded, the wound had knitted and the stitches had gone. It had been less serious than it had seemed. The horn had gouged a six inch gash along Guy's side but it had been very shallow.

Jessica shuddered to herself when she thought of how it could have been much more terrible. When she had seen the way in which the blood had poured out, she had believed that Guy was close to death. Her terror had brought home to her how much she felt for him.

The first visit to the hospital, once Guy had recovered from the sedative, had been curiously stilted. She had thanked him again for saving Roberta's life. The little girl had recovered quite remarkably from the fright and had basked in the clucking concern of the Tibetan women.

Jessica had heard her daughter chatting happily to them in what sounded like a mixture of English and Urdu and, amazingly, Jessica had understood some of the Urdu. She had continued to plough away at the taped lessons as much as she could and was able to converse slowly and carefully in the simplest terms with Wazir Khan as well as the Tibetans.

Jessica soaped her left leg thoughtfully. Guy had been so defensive, she recalled, when she had visited him. He had shrugged off her thanks and been more concerned about thanking her. Jessica had become equally off-hand.

'Wazir Khan was the one who did all the work,' she said.

'That's not the way he tells it,' Guy answered, 'which is something for a Pathan.' His smile had appeared like a sunbeam. 'Mind you, his own part is not understated.' He shook his head. 'He's been preening himself for days. One of the nurses is Indian so she got the full story and passed it on. Even that vinegar-faced one has started to thaw.'

He laughed. 'I'm only glad he didn't decide to slaughter the bull while he was about it. That would have cost a bit. It's a pedigree animal. Has a pedigree temper as well,' he added thoughtfully.

'He's not the only one with a temper,' Jessica put in teasingly.

Guy opened his eyes wide. 'You're not referring to me, I hope?' he asked with dignity.

Jessica returned his stare with a grin. 'As if I would,' she said and reached out for his hand.

'As I recall,' Guy said after an interval, 'the beef curry on legs episode rudely interrupted an interesting conversation.'

She looked enquiringly at him.

'You were talking about a certain Friday evening,' he reminded her gently.

Jessica blushed. 'Oh, that,' she said, trying to sound unconcerned, 'yes.'

'Yes, what?' Guy's voice was teasing. He paused. 'You were saying, I think,' he prompted, 'that you weren't objecting.'

Jessica lowered her eyes. 'I wasn't.'

'You did struggle a little,' he said, slyly amused.

'I didn't, I was unbalanced!' she retorted indignantly.

'I certainly was,' Guy murmured. He shifted slightly in the bed, wincing with the effort.

The nurse had entered before he could say anymore and Jessica had retreated, her heart pounding.

She did have good legs, Jessica reassured herself as she started on the right one. They were elegantly long. If she wore the black dress with the thin shoulder straps this evening, she could utilise the black shoes, with the three inches of stiletto heel that did so much to shape her legs into graceful curves.

Guy had become enthusiastic whenever the conversation had turned to the orphanage and hospital in India. He had been excited about the stamps and they speculated happily about how much they might fetch. Jessica had spoken to Mr Wilkins a few days after the accident and he had hinted, cautiously, that they could realise even more than he had suggested. It was as certain as anything could be that the trust fund would become a reality.

'What's more,' Guy said happily, 'there'll be enough to carry out some of my plans for the estate,' His face had become pensive, then cheerful. 'I'll be able to make it a proper wildlife haven and let people have proper access to it.'

'Won't it spoil the privacy?' Jessica asked quietly.

Guy had smiled. 'Privileges also give responsibility,' he rejoined. He shifted in the bed. 'My ribs sometimes itch rotten,' he had grumbled, 'underneath the bandages and I can't do a thing about it.' He had hesitated. 'Do you think you could scratch my side, very, very, gently?' he asked.

Sensation streamed up her fingers and along her arm when he rolled awkwardly to one side and she had pulled back his pyjama jacket to put her hand on his skin.

She had taken the greatest of care, moving her hand softly, trying to prolong the intimacy of the moment. Her fingers had lingered and Guy had moved back to his original position with muttered thanks.

'I won't open all the estate,' he had continued. 'I don't want people trampling over the badger sett for one thing,' he went on. 'Brock has been there for near enough a thousand years and I reckon he's entitled to go on that way in decent privacy.' He had shrugged and winced as he did so. 'No, it all needs careful planning,' he said, 'and I'll have the money with which to do it thanks to Jessica Tankerton's boy friend.'

'He was rather more than a boy friend,' Jessica said. 'I've been reading her diaries.' She had gone on to tell him just a little about what she had discovered. Somehow, she felt a reluctance to reveal everything she had learned about the old lady who spoke across the years through her journal.

She would wear her hair long and loose, she decided. The black tresses would be allowed to tumble down onto her shoulders, mingling with the black string shoulderstraps of the dress. She would wear the discreet gold pendant earrings that she had found in a little antique shop in London. They would be hidden much of the time but, occasionally as the light struck and her hair swayed, they would gleam softly.

Guy had breathed a great sigh of satisfaction when he came back to Tankerton Hall from the hospital. Jessica and Wazir Khan had helped him climb the steps that led to the front door. He had stood in the hallway for long, ticking seconds before turning to her, the blue eyes strangely still.

'Thank you, Jessica,' he said quietly before he leaned forward and kissed her gently on the mouth.

The touch of his lips sent a pulsebeat of excitement through her and she returned the pressure of his lips, wanting to throw her arms about him and resisting, conscious of his wounded side.

'I don't want to rush.' His voice was very soft. 'Can you accept that?'

She nodded.

Jessica had no more doubts about how she felt about Guy. She liked him, found him fun to be with, knew that it was not merely a physical attraction that brought her to his side, not simple desire that peppered her thoughts with images of him, but a need that pushed the physical attraction into perspective, making it part of an overall relationship. Piers and Jessica Tankerton both, they knew what love should be. Piers because he had never experienced it, old Jessica because she had.

Jessica got out of the bath carefully and wrapped herself in a towel. The few days that had passed since Guy returned to the Hall had been peculiarly frustrating but she was content to let Guy take his time. Each day she went to the library but there was rarely any sign of him. He even failed to appear for lunch most days and she mentioned it to Wazir Khan.

The Pathan had spoken confidingly to her, in a mixture of Urdu and his peculiar English which he had picked up from the films he adored. 'Sahib Guy is thinking, memsahib, very deep thoughts. He is realising, I think, what others can already see.' He shrugged. 'If the damned bull had been quicker or this damned Pathan slower, no more Tankyton people.' His face had split in a wide grin. 'Threatened to kick me when I tell him what to do. Calls me donkey with the mind of tomcat. Bloody fine compliment.'

Roberta was with Wazir Khan now. Jessica dried herself carefully and walked, unclothed, to the bedroom. It was lovely the way Roberta had developed because of the Tibetans and Wazir Khan. From what Jessica could gather, Roberta was rapidly becoming a person of wonder and mystery at school. Not every five year old could speak loftily of a Pathan babysitter!

Jessica looked at her watch. She had two hours to spare. She sat down at her dressing table and began to brush her hair, long strokes which burnished the coal-black length of it to a glistening sheen. Guy's invitation had come out of the blue. He had walked into the library, jauntily, cockily, in command. She had smiled an automatic greeting.

'How would you like dinner with me tonight?' he said. 'By way of celebration because I'm in full working order once more. To thank you for everything you've done, to toast the success of the auction when it happens, anything you like.'

He studied his fingernails and his voice was determinedly casual. 'It would probably be as easy for you and Roberta to spend the night at the Hall,' he said carefully, 'the Tibs will be pretty busy and dinner might go on rather. We may have a lot to talk about.' He coughed, seeming embarrassed.

Jessica smiled. 'I'd love to,' she said warmly, 'have dinner, I mean and sample your hospitality overnight.'

His eyes seemed to bore into her soul and she felt her knees tremble for the fraction of a second.

Guy nodded. 'I shall drag my cream dinner jacket out of retirement,' he said, 'and dazzle you with the whitest of shirts. Be a good idea to wear dark glasses.'

That was one other reason why she had chosen the black. It would be a complete contrast. She inspected her hair. It looked good. Jessica stood and dusted talcum powder over herself carefully. Her make-up would be precise and discreet, enhancing her oval face, emphasising the long eyelashes, high cheekbones and the full lips.

She inspected herself in the mirror before she pulled on the black dress. She was still defiantly slim and she knew that her body could tantalise. She shivered again at the thought of his touch and her tongue flickered, moistening lips that were suddenly dry with expectation.

Guy had suggested with the faintest hint of command that Roberta stayed at the Hall for tea. The Tibetans would look after her and, he had said casually, she might like to take the rest of the afternoon off so that she could get ready without rushing. She had to be interpreting his words correctly, Jessica reassured herself carefully.

She looked at her watch. It was time to leave. She looked round the cottage with a stranger's eyes before walking steadily out to her car. It was only a few hundred yards to the Hall but she would not risk arriving windswept. She got in carefully, ensuring that the dress did not crush, and started the engine with a deliberate movement, knowing that she was about to commit herself to Guy Tankerton.

Wazir Khan was standing by the door when she arrived, dressed in his finery. He looked like an exotically plumed bird and his head bowed briefly as she walked up the steps to the front entrance of the Hall.

'Memsahib.'

'Wazir Khan.'

He turned and walked in front of her, silent, wraith-like, leading the way to the dining room, taking her down the corridor she knew so well but which had somehow turned into a long passageway of invitation. His tap on the door was brief and she walked past him into the room and stopped, drawing her breath in sharply as the door closed silently behind her.

The room had been transformed. There was no harsh electric light, just the soft glow of candle flames. The air was thick with the scent of jasmine, frangipani, mimosa, perfumed incense curling its way upwards in lazy spirals of thin smoke, adding a languorous excitement to the atmosphere. The dinner table was without a cloth, set with silver which was reflected in the polished oak surface. Tubby candles, supported by blossoms, floated in shallow silver bowls filled with water, the flickering light sending shadows dancing across the gleaming cutlery and dishes on the dark wooden table.

Guy walked forward. He was impeccably dressed and Jessica's heart lurched as she studied him. The cream jacket, short-waisted, clung to him like a second skin and he was wearing dark trousers, cut tight, which followed the line of his legs with calculated precision. His hand came out, took hers, and she welcomed the surge of happiness that ran through her at the touch of his fingers.

They ate in almost complete silence. Guy spoke inconsequentially as Wazir Khan moved silently to and fro. The Pathan faded into the background after each course had been served, pausing only to replenish the wine-glasses at their side.

Jessica's heart thudded inside her as time ticked past. Guy's face was shadowed in the candle light, the golden glow from the flames picking out the chiselled angles of his face. She could hardly guess at the dishes. Each one was a new and wonderful sensation and the end of the meal came with a superb confection of fresh fruits, fruits that she could not even identify. Wazir Khan poured coffee and inclined his head gravely.

'Thank you, Wazir Khan,' Guy said in Urdu. 'You have done well.' It was, Jessica knew, a formal compliment.

Guy did not speak for long moments after the butler had left.

Jessica studied him, wondering if she should break the silence.

Guy's eyes were dark indigo pools in the half light. 'We must talk,' he said carefully, 'there is something we must discuss.'

Jessica nodded, her head moving the merest fraction.

'Once upon a time,' Guy began, 'there was someone who meant a great deal to me. I asked her to marry me.'

Jessica inclined her head, holding her silence but she wanted to cry out to him to forget the past, to seize the present, take her into his life.

'I knew,' Guy said carefully, 'that some things which I held dear were of little importance to her. She could not understand, perhaps did not wish to understand, that I straddled two cultures.'

Just as Jessica Tankerton had done, she thought. The journal had revealed more and more of what the old lady had believed and Guy was closer to her than he realised.

'I thought,' Guy continued in the same quiet, deliberate tones, 'that she might come to care for the things that I held dear.' His face was impassive. 'Even if she did not, I did not care for I loved her dearly. She was the sun and the moon in the heavens, the stars in the sky and the wind in the trees to me.'

Jessica lowered her eyes. She must show no sign, make no comment. Guy was at his most vulnerable as he spoke about the woman he had once loved.

'She thought it amusing that I should be as I am,' Guy said slowly, 'she thought it strange that I should be as bhai-bund with Wazir Khan, she thought it pointless that I should give a home to my Tibetans, an extravagance that I should concern myself with an orphanage eight thousand miles away.'

Jessica raised her eyes to stare at him. He was not looking at her, but staring into the distance, feeling afresh the pain of the memories.

'Yet I continued to love her, hoping, believing, that she would one day understand.' The smile that twisted across his lips like a phantom was sad and bitter. 'She never did and one day she told me that she had found someone else, someone who was fun to be with,' Guy said with slow, dragging words, 'and then she laughed and added, it was someone who wouldn't waste her time with Indians and orphans.'

Jessica gazed at him steadily and at last his head turned and he looked at her.

'When I first saw you,' he said, 'my heart came to life again. Each time I spoke to you, I felt a happiness that I thought had perished. It was enough to be near you.' He smiled softly, tenderly now. 'I believed that you were still in love with a memory of Justin.'

The name came as a shock, the past had receded so far in the last days. She shook her head very slowly. Justin had been part of another life, a life she had led before she met Guy.

'Then,' he went on slowly, 'I thought that you were attracted to Piers. That hurt. I was blind and stupid, selfish about it, because I had fallen in love with you.' His words lingered on the scented air.

Jessica fought to still the trembling in her limbs. She rose, slowly, and walked round the table to where Guy sat. She sank to her knees and lowered her head, put her hands together in a gesture of submission and spoke in a low voice.

She had practised the words again and again, preparing for this moment, knowing it would come.

'Mai aapsar pyar karthihu,' Jessica whispered, her voice trembling. 'I love you.'

His hands came forward with slow deliberation and he pushed back the dark hair that had fallen forward as she bowed her head.

His fingers framed her face with the soft touch of butterfly wings. 'You understand the implications of what you have just said?' His words were a throaty murmur. 'You understand you are offering yourself to me as a wife?' He sounded disbelieving.

She nodded, mute, and lowered her head again, keeping her hands together.

'My princess,' Guy said, 'my love, my pearl, you have conquered my heart and I am honoured that you wish me to be your husband!' His voice was a soft murmur, hanging in the scented air, full of love and pride.

His hands moved to encompass her and he pulled lightly, urging her silently to her feet. The flickering candles sent shafts of golden light shimmering through the aromatic air of the dining room, gleaming as they bounced off the crystal and silver dishes.

Jessica stood, silent, as he faced her. His hands moved slowly, deliberately to her bare shoulders and she trembled with excitement as he plunged his fingers into her dark hair.

Guy pulled her to him, tilting her head, and her lips opened in welcome as he pressed his mouth down onto hers. She clung desperately to him, her blood pounding as his lips crushed her own with a gentle persistence. His hands were warm against her bare back and a long tremulous shudder passed through her as his fingers moved, slowly, intently, purposefully across her flesh.

'I love you,' he whispered urgently, 'I love you, Jessica, my princess.'

'I love you,' she murmured in a

passionate return of his words, turning her mouth up to his again in a swift desire to taste the honey of his lips once more.

His hands stroked her forehead.

'My precious heart,' Guy whispered, 'we belong together. I know we do.' He took her hands in his. 'You have made me very happy,' he murmured softly and his blue eyes looked deep into hers. 'All I can ask now,' he said with the faintest twitch of laughter on his lips, 'is when do you want to marry me?'

Jessica returned the pressure of his fingers.

'As soon as it can be arranged,' she answered in a low whisper, 'for I love you and I must be with you.' She looked up in to his face, shadowed in the flickering light of the candles and felt a sighing wave of contentment flow over her.

He kissed her again at the door to her room. 'You have made me so happy, so proud. I shall always love you.' His voice was a soft sigh of contentment.

She was still asleep when the thumping knock at the door woke her. Jessica stirred sleepily and called out a yawned invitation to enter.

It was Wazir Khan. His face was a cheerful grin as he strode across the room followed by a giggling Tibetan girl carrying an armful of garments. Jessica watched, open-mouthed, as the Pathan carefully supervised the Tibetan as she hung up two of Jessica's dresses, put away a selection of underwear in a drawer and carefully placed Jessica's dressing gown by the bedside.

Guy's voice came to her from the doorway. He was already dressed in sweater and slacks. 'I hope you didn't mind us raiding the cottage,' he said casually, 'because I'd rather like you to stay here from now on.' His voice was assured. He stood to one side as Wazir Khan and the Tibetan left. 'When you're dressed,' Guy continued, 'we'll discuss plans.' His face was suddenly worried. 'Unless you have already thought better of it,' he added tentatively.

'Not a chance,' Jessica smiled at him from over the bed cover. 'You're trapped, Guy Tankerton, so you may as well get used to the idea!'

Guy came back when she had almost finished dressing. He put his head round the door, a broad smile on his face.

'I'm sorry about this,' he said, 'not the ideal circumstances. I really ought to go down on one knee and hold a bunch of flowers.' His blue eyes were dancing with amusement. 'I fear, Jessica Blair, you are just going to have to marry me as soon as possible.'

Jessica stared at him.

'You don't have any choice in the matter,' Guy went on, his lean face grave, 'it's out of my hands!'

Jessica looked at him, completely bewildered.

'What are you talking about?' she asked.

Guy sighed. 'I'm a lost man,' he said and began to chuckle softly. 'Wazir Khan,' he said in a precise whisper, 'is very determinedly cleaning your shoes!'

10

'Mummy,' asked Roberta thoughtfully, 'are we going to live with Uncle Guy and Wazir for always?' She was sitting up in bed and looked about her happily. 'I've never had a room as nice as this before,' she commented gleefully, 'and Teddy likes it too.' The little girl hugged the soft toy firmly to her.

Jessica stroked her daughter's hair. 'Yes, darling,' she said as the warm glow that suffused her since that magical night bubbled up again, 'we are staying here for always.'

Roberta gave a satisfied nod. 'Will Uncle Guy become my Daddy one day?' she asked.

Jessica felt helpless, wondering how to explain the wonderful, miraculous events to a little girl who had never known her real father. 'He will be like a Daddy,' she began cautiously, 'but your real Daddy — ' She broke off.

Roberta looked at her. 'Wazir says that Uncle Guy will be bhai-bundi to me,' she said, 'and that an Infinite Wisdom has chosen him to take the place of Daddy-who-died.' She mixed the English and Urdu phrases without concern. 'He said that it sometimes takes a very long time to find the best bhai-bundi and that karma cannot be hurried.' She snuggled down into the bed. 'Night night, Mummy,' she said sleepily.

Thank you, Wazir Khan, Jessica thought as she kissed Roberta's cheek. She sat by the bed while Roberta drifted into sleep. It seemed years ago that she had been living a routine life in London. She could never have guessed what would happen as a result of changing her job. A Pathan butler and Tibetan servants, it all sounded so exotic and yet she had adapted so readily. The Hall was home, she knew that in the very depths of her being and she had no doubts that she and Guy were destined to be together.

'In ten days time,' Guy said precisely when she rejoined him downstairs, 'we get married.' He looked round the lounge. 'In this very room, in fact.'

'I know that,' Jessica said, 'what about it?'

'What happens after the ceremony?' Guy asked.

'Well,' Jessica began with a smirk, 'once we've got rid of the guests, we make a bee-line for the bedroom and — '

'I didn't mean that precisely,' Guy broke in with dignity, 'I was thinking rather more of where than of what.' He relaxed in his chair. 'Honeymoon, albeit must be belated,' he explained succinctly and yawned elaborately. 'Where else, but the great sub-continent of India?' he asked rhetorically.

Jessica went to his side and sat on the arm of the chair. 'When do we go?' she asked eagerly, 'and for how long?'

'Hang on,' Guy said patiently. His

fingers feathered across her shoulder. 'After the auction,' he answered, 'and we'll travel about, but most of all we go to the orphanage to hand over the money and let you see where Jessica Tankerton spent some of her time because you're going to write about her, and we'll probably be away for six weeks.' He paused for breath. 'Was that everything?' he asked. His lips brushed her cheek.

'What about Roberta?'

'That depends on you,' Guy said, 'but I think it's probably better if she stays here. The Tibs will spoil her rotten, of course, but that can't be helped.' He kissed her cheek. 'We'll make it up to her later, I promise'.

'It sounds wonderful,' Jessica said thoughtfully. She was going to miss Roberta desperately. Six weeks was a long time to be away and Roberta would be very lonely on her own.

'Darling, it will be our honeymoon,' Guy chided softly, reading her thoughts. 'I find Roberta charming but I honestly don't think that it would be right for her to be travelling around India at her age.'

'Is Wazir coming as well?' Jessica said, slightly brittle. 'If he is, he could look after her.' She wouldn't be able to explain to Roberta why she and Guy were abandoning her. Panic gripped her. She could not leave her daughter for that long. Roberta had not spent a day of her life without her near.

Guy gave a soft sigh. 'Wazir will be flying out with us,' he said, 'and will go off to see his people. We'll meet up again shortly before we return. It's his holiday, Jessica,' he explained patiently, 'he goes back every couple of years.' He sat up. 'Did you seriously believe he would trail round with us?' he questioned, 'a fine honeymoon that would be!'

'I didn't know.' Jessica heard the sharpness in her voice. 'I haven't had the advantage of being brought up surrounded by hordes of servants. I don't know the etiquette on these occasions.' Guy was being stupidly obtuse if he couldn't understand that she must make sure Roberta was happy.

'Don't be so nonsensical,' Guy said, his voice starting to crackle with anger, 'that's got nothing to do with it.'

Jessica's vision blurred as tears prickled her eyes. 'You're right,' she said miserably and sniffed. 'It's just the thought of being away from Roberta for so long and I'm sure you're right about it because she might get ill and it would be a constant worry but I know I shall miss her so much. I'm sorry.'

'So am I.' Guy's voice was gentle. 'We shouldn't quarrel about anything,' he said, 'not even the tiniest of spats because it hurts too much.' He moved, putting his arm round her. 'There's only one way to solve the problem,' he murmured, 'we'll just have to ask Roberta!'

Jessica was working in the library the next morning when Guy breezed in. 'Never under-estimate the guile of

Pathans and little girls,' he announced cheerfully.

Jessica eyed him cautiously.

'I mentioned the problem to Wazir Khan,' Guy said, 'the little difference we had about Roberta.' He took her hand. 'Wazir Khan, with an innocence that would make a new born baby seem a reprobate suggested that he went home a month before we travel.' He stopped.

'Yes?' Jessica prompted.

Guy gave a smile. 'Wazir Khan has a cousin,' he explained with precision. 'A female cousin. It is Wazir Khan's opinion that he and the said female would be able to look after Roberta quite happily. He would travel up country, acquire the cousin and then meet us at the airport when we arrived. Roberta is enthralled at the idea of coming with us and the pair of them probably discussed it in detail beforehand.' He smiled. 'I suspect Wazir has already filled her head with tales of the mysterious East.

There will be tantrums if we don't agree.'

'Roberta doesn't throw tantrums,' Jessica said, leaping to her child's defence.

'Wazir Khan does, though,' Guy said mournfully. His voice softened. 'There is more to the cousin than meets the eye, I think,' he said carefully, 'he hopped about a bit when I asked a few questions. Very evasive.'

Jessica smiled. 'It sounds the perfect answer, and I don't think I would have the heart to stand between Wazir Khan and a female cousin.'

'Good.' Guy kissed her. He studied her for a moment. 'Are you going to carry on working after you are married?' he asked with a sudden grin.

Jessica opened her eyes in surprise. 'My husband-to-be and I haven't discussed it,' she said primly and her toes curled as he put his arms about her and kissed her again. 'I shall do whatever he wishes,' she said breathlessly when he released her.

'Mind you do,' Guy warned, 'nothing upsets a man more than a self-willed wife!'

'How very romantic of you to say so!'

'I am a romantic, actually,' Guy said, faint indignation colouring his words. 'I think it would be good for this house to have a Jessica Tankerton in residence once more.'

'That reminds me,' Jessica said practically, 'I must start work on the book about her. You can help actually, my darling.'

Guy put up his hands in a gesture of surrender. 'I can't write,' he denied.

'Family history,' Jessica said, ignoring his protest. 'How did Jessica come by a niece? You never mentioned that she had any brothers or sisters.'

'She didn't.'

'In which case.' Jessica said, 'it's rather difficult for her to have a great-niece.'

'Slapdash family way of speaking,' Guy said. 'The child was Lord Tankerton's great-niece. Jessica's father, the one who built this place, had an elder brother who also served in India, married there and produced a son. He must have been a few years older than Jessica but he's not important really. He was in the Indian Army. He married and a daughter blessed that particular union.'

'I see,' Jessica said. 'That was the great-niece who was actually, what, second cousin to Jessica Tankerton?'

'Absolutely,' Guy said, 'and Jessica raised her as it happened. It was all very fortuitous. Jessica was out in India at the time apparently, round about 1870 or so, I guess. There was a cholera epidemic and the cousin and his wife died at some remote post up-country. The story goes that Jessica got a telegram and travelled miles and miles to rescue the little girl who was only a baby. The old duck brought her home to England.'

He grinned. 'I don't know why I'm telling you all this,' he said, 'it's all in the family Bible which is kept in here anyway.' He frowned. 'I'd thought you had old Jessica's diaries. It must be mentioned in there.'

'Darling,' Jessica said patiently, 'they are very thick volumes with lots of tiny writing and I just dipped into them. I must admit I cheated. The writing gets bigger when she is much older and is easier to read. Eyesight failing, I suppose.'

Guy found the Bible for her, gave her another kiss, and went off. Jessica sat down and looked at the family tree that was written inside the front cover. It was just as Guy had described it. She felt a vague sense of disappointment that there was no mention of a William anywhere. Jessica's cousin, who had been swept away by cholera was Rodney and his wife, whose sole memorial Jessica realised was probably the fading entry in front of her, was named Victoria. Named after the old Queen, without a doubt, Jessica thought automatically. The baby, the child that Jessica had rescued, was called Camilla.

She studied the details once more. Jessica Tankerton had lived until 1917, five years after the journal entry about William. It would be a matter of going very steadily and carefully through all the diaries. William must be mentioned somewhere else in there. So much had happened since she had read that entry, Jessica thought ruefully, so much wonder and joy had come into her life, that she had neglected to do the most elementary research. She made a firm decision. After lunch, she would start on the trail of Jessica Tankerton's Indian lover!

There was no doubt about it, Jessica realised four hours later, some diaries were missing. She rubbed her hand across her eyes wearily. There had to be some other volumes elsewhere. Either that or Jessica Tankerton just did not trouble to keep one when she went off on her travels. That seemed odd because the old lady had kept them meticulously day by day. Jessica had found the entries had stopped in the middle of 1869. The ones just before the break were full of her plans and excitement at travelling out to the East once more.

Jessica had waded through masses of minute detail and then discovered the diaries broke off for two years and resumed as if there had been no hiatus. The only way of picking out the date was to examine Jessica's crabbed handwriting carefully and it had taken her several minutes to realise what had happened. She had seen Camilla's name and it had been a few moments before she worked out that the entry had been resumed without a break. Jessica studied the entry again:

September 3rd, 1872 A Long Journey from Southampton but Baby did Well. Each Time I look upon her I Cannot but Wonder at The Workings of Divine Providence. Tho' it is Hard to Contemplate Such Things, it does Seem that the Carrying Off of Poor

Rodney and His Family was a Blessing In Disguise. I Think It is My Duty to Ensure that She is Baptised into the Christian Faith. The Name is Camilla.'

The child must have been very young when her parents died, Jessica reasoned. She studied the entry once more, trying to search out the slightest clue. There was something odd about it, something that was just sitting on the edges of her brain, an inconsistency that nagged gently at her.

With sudden resolution, she went to the trunks of family papers and she had just finished a fruitless search when Guy walked in to the library office.

'You look hot, bothered and dusty,' he said with a smile, 'hunting for more rare stamps?'

Jessica explained that there were some diaries missing.

Guy shrugged carelessly.

'They will be important, I'm sure,' Jessica said earnestly. She frowned. There was something odd about the first mention of Camilla.

'They might be anywhere,' Guy said, 'this place is a rabbit warren, darling. If she kept her Indian stuff separately, it might even have been destroyed after she died.'

'Yes,' Jessica said thoughtfully, 'I suppose so.' She smiled. 'I wish I knew what she looked like.'

Guy looked surprised. 'That's easy,' he said. 'There's a whole batch of paintings which I took down when I moved in. Most needed cleaning and I haven't got around to having them done. They're stacked away in an empty room.' He gave a shudder. 'Pretty desperate mostly,' he added, 'various Tankertons from days of yore posing by heaps of dead birds or animals. Very depressing. There are some photograph albums somewhere as well,' he said, 'probably stuffed in a cupboard in here, I expect. I remember looking through them as a kid.'

He gave a soft, reminiscing smile and Jessica's heart thumped. She did love him so much. 'Great entertainment on wet Sunday afternoons, guess who was hiding under the face fungus.' His blue eyes glowed. 'Fancy me with a beard?' he asked lightly.

'I fancy you all the time,' Jessica answered happily. She gazed round the library. Every bookcase had a cupboard underneath it. 'I'll start looking for the albums,' she said.

'Tomorrow,' Guy answered firmly, 'it's time we gave Roberta some attention.' He kissed her cheek softly. 'And time you thought of me,' he grumbled gently, 'not dear old Jessica the First. I'm sure she won't mind waiting. I promise we'll find her portrait tomorrow.'

Guy staggered into the library the next morning with the painting of Jessica Tankerton. He put it down and examined it critically. 'It looks a bit like her,' he said, 'if you find a photograph, you'll be able to compare it.' He sniffed. 'It's not exactly great art,' he opined, 'and that round thing

233

with legs is presumably the niece.'

'What lovely earrings!' Jessica exclaimed at once. She gazed at the painting intently. Jessica Tankerton was blonde and had blue eyes, the same blue that she saw in Guy's. It was the earrings Jessica Tankerton was wearing, though, that leapt out of the portrait. Long dangling golden pendants, each ending in a ruby, as large and as red as ripening cherries.

'Trust a woman to notice something like that,' Guy observed idly. 'They are splendid, though,' he agreed, 'Indian without a doubt. Probably loot from the Mutiny brought back by her father. I suppose we should stick it up somewhere,' he said.

Jessica did not reply. The portrait wasn't very good really, it was almost primitive and had probably been done by a local artist. He had captured, nonetheless, a shrewdness in the features and, Jessica thought with a sudden flash of excitement, a worldliness, a sexual awareness which seemed to bounce out of the picture. Jessica Tankerton, she realised with sudden insight, had been a voluptuous woman, a woman who had loved and been loved. There was a physical, earthy spirit peeping out from the staid Victorian costume.

Camilla, standing by her aunt's side, looked about three years old which meant the picture was painted about 1875. It was interesting, Jessica thought as she studied the picture, that it was Camilla who had, even allowing for the inadequacies of the artist and childhood plumpness, the family resemblance which was found in Guy. There were the signs of the sharp face that she loved so much.

'Well?' Guy said.

'Sorry?'

'Do we stick it up somewhere?'

'We'll do it next week,' Jessica answered after a moment's thought. She linked her arm through Guy's. 'We'll put it on the wall in here, my love, the day that another Jessica Tankerton becomes resident at the Hall!'

11

'One million, four hundred thousand pounds,' Guy said yet again in an awed voice, 'and that's after commission fees!' He shook his head in slow wonder before looking up at the portrait of the first Jessica. 'Definitely a cleaning for you,' he said, 'founder of the family fortunes and restorer of them after a century and a half!'

Jessica threw her arms around him. 'I'm so pleased and happy,' she said, her eyes sparkling, 'it's absolutely marvellous!'

Guy beamed at Jessica. 'This calls for a celebration,' he declared, 'I'll root out some champagne.'

'At four o'clock in the afternoon?' Jessica laughed, 'we should save it for this evening.'

Guy's face twitched. 'We might be celebrating in a rather more personal fashion later,' he suggested.

Jessica raised her eyebrows. 'I knew I shouldn't have married you,' she said, teasing gently, 'you're always pestering me for your marital rights.'

Guy hugged her. 'Darling Jessica,' he murmured, 'making love must always be a mutual desire. If ever you agree just because you believe it is what I want, I would never forgive you.'

Jessica returned the pressure of his embrace. 'I know that, my prince,' she whispered in soft reply, 'and I was teasing you. You are so kind and considerate, never pressurising me, always understanding.' She stroked his hair. 'You're very crafty,' she accused softly, 'because it just increases my love for you and so I want to express it to you more and more often.'

'Damn,' Guy answered, 'you've guessed my cunning plan.' He was jubilant, excitement chasing across his face as he held her. 'One million, four hundred thousand,' he breathed again. He pulled away, holding her at arm's-length. 'It's full steam ahead for our honeymoon, my darling,' he said. 'Wazir Khan is ready to go and we'll follow in five weeks from now. It won't be too stinking hot as it will be September before we get there and, in any event, we'll be up in the hills for much of the time. In fact,' he smiled, 'you'll probably feel cold.'

Jessica bit her lip. 'Roberta will miss school,' she said practically. 'If we're away six weeks, we won't be back until it's almost November.'

Guy looked surprised. 'Far be it from me to criticise teachers,' he replied, 'but I think this trip might be better for her than making mud pies or whatever it is they do at infant school these days.' He shook his head in mock exasperation. 'Darling, she speaks English and Urdu, reads like a Shakespearean scholar, and has a computerlike calculating ability if her negotiations with me over her pocket money are any guide. Do you know,' he demanded, 'she claimed an extra fifty pence a week because she wants to save money to buy Pathan clothes in India? She has a brain like a whetted scalpel. Missing school won't harm her, take my word for it.'

'I suppose so,' Jessica said reluctantly, 'and she's reading because I encourage her.' She chuckled. 'Her financial acumen comes from Wazir Khan, I overheard him putting her up to it.' She shook her head affectionately as she looked at Guy. 'You're right as usual, you pig,' she said without rancour.

'Husbands always are,' Guy answered smugly. He pulled her to him. 'You haven't even asked where we are going in India.'

Jessica bared her teeth. 'I wouldn't dare, O mighty one,' she teased with exaggerated humility, 'what am I but a feeble woman, unable to think or reason, and certainly not equipped to question such a superior being as yourself?'

Guy hugged her. 'Keep it up,' he said, 'you're learning.' He let out a yell as Jessica nipped the lobe of his ear with her fingers. 'All right,' he confessed hastily, 'I give in!'

'Good,' Jessica said firmly. She gave a dazzling smile. 'Champagne to celebrate and you tell me where we are going,' she said. 'That's if I'm allowed to stop work for the day,' she finished with a laugh.

'We fly out to Delhi,' Guy began when he had poured their drinks, 'and we'll spend a month sight-seeing, the full tourist bit. The Taj Mahal, elephants with howdahs, all that stuff, but we eventually end up near a place called Dharmsala.' He took a gulp of champagne. 'The orphanage is about ten miles outside the town, in its own grounds. It's quite close to the border so we have to be circumspect. It's totally non-political and both sides accept it.'

Jessica looked at him, curiosity in her eyes.

Guy gave a soft sigh. 'I'm not going to get on my high horse,' he said, 'but back before India and Pakistan became independent, the whole sub-continent was a single unit in the British Empire. The bureaucrats drew a pencil line which ruled off the bottom two-thirds. That became India, the remainder became Pakistan. India is mainly Hindu, Pakistan mainly Moslem and the enmity between those two faiths has existed for a thousand years. Kashmir itself,' Guy went on in careful tones, 'is in a sort of corner between China, Tibet and Afghanistan. The population is Moslem but it was ruled for five hundred years by Hindu princes so both countries claim it.'

He wandered over to a chair and sat down. 'Ever since 1947,' he went on, acid creeping into his words, 'they've been squabbling about it, camping their damned armies in it, fighting, killing, and the poor bloody population has had to take it on the chin.' His tones had become vehement. 'Kashmir is probably the most beautiful country in the world,' he explained and then he grinned, 'with the most beautiful women in the world, come to that,' he added, 'and now there are segments of the local population who want both India and Pakistan to go away and let Kashmir look after itself and they've got violent about it as well. So there's more shooting, more killing, more wounding, and we have more kids without parents, more children without arms or legs or both.'

'It sounds awfully dangerous,' Jessica said anxiously, 'are you sure Roberta will be all right?'

'She — We — will be fine,' Guy said in instant reassurance. 'I told you, we keep our noses out of local affairs and everyone respects us for it.' His smile was comforting. 'The orphanage and hospital have been there for over one hundred years, darling, and thanks to Jessica the First, are likely to remain so for another century.' He moved back to her. 'It really is lovely there,' he said enthusiastically, 'you wake up in the morning and look across through the clear air, towards Nepal and you can see the Himalayas rising up into a blue sky like gigantic frozen waves or a wedding cake gone wrong.' He stopped as Jessica tensed. 'I'm sorry,' he apologised after a moment of reflection, 'Justin was killed there, wasn't he?'

Jessica nodded. 'Don't fret yourself, darling,' she responded slowly, 'it was just that it seems so strange to think that I will be able to see the mountains on which he died.' She shook her head. 'You speak about India so casually, and I take everything for granted as well, and yet six years ago, it sounded and seemed like the other side of eternity. I never dreamed that I'd actually go there.' She pressed his hands. 'Darling Guy, don't fret,' she repeated, 'I'm not mourning yesterday's ghost.'

Jessica thought she had stepped completely naked into a gigantic oven when she followed Guy down the aircraft steps at Delhi Airport. The heat grasped her in a giant, sweaty fist. Roberta clung tightly to her hand as they were ferried to the arrivals hall, filled with customs and immigration officers and a seething crowd that could be glimpsed beyond the desks of the officials. A babble of noise hit her ears as she kept close to Guy while they completed the arrival formalities. It was utterly bewildering, Jessica thought to herself. Her feet were tired, swollen after the long flight, she was trying hard not to fall asleep and everything was so exciting she didn't want to miss a single moment of it! Her nostrils twitched as a bewildering assortment of exciting smells and perfumes came to her. She couldn't identify any of them with certainty yet there was a vigour, a pulsating life about them. She stared about her as they moved into the throng of faces. Everywhere she looked there were women in saris and shalwars, colours ranging from gold and silver to blues and reds, men in a bewildering variety of different clothes, western suits, turbans and pantaloons with coloured shirts.

There was a minor eruption in the

mob and Wazir Khan appeared, trailed by two sad looking porters.

'Memsahib, Missy memsahib,' Wazir Khan said, 'I have the spawn of a single camel dropping waiting with a shameful jalopy he calls a taxi.'

She really could understand him without thinking about it, Jessica realised with amazement. In the last weeks, she and Guy had often spoken in Urdu rather than English and, even though she was not completely fluent, she had discovered she could switch with increasing ease into the language.

The woman standing by the taxi was quite the loveliest Jessica had ever seen. Dressed in a simple shalwar, she waited motionless by the taxi towards which Wazir Khan led them. He turned as they reached the car and Jessica saw the look of pride on his face.

'Sahib,' he said formally, 'my bhai-bundi, Zaheena, my wife.' He gestured to the porters. 'Load the cases into this wretched excuse for a vehicle,' he commanded in a rattling Urdu as Guy and Jessica gaped at him. Wazir Khan turned back with a sheepish grin on his face. 'It was time,' he said loftily, 'and she is a good Pathan.'

In the month that followed, Jessica came to appreciate why Guy was so enchanted with India; why the first Jessica had gone back, time and time again. Roberta seemed to be utterly at home and she and Zaheena chattered and played happily for hours.

There was never any worry about leaving her daughter if she and Guy were going off somewhere which would not interest the little girl because Wazir Khan and Zaheena looked after her with an incredible devotion and Roberta was absurdly proud when she was mistaken for a Pathan child. Jessica caught her one day, happily trading insults in Urdu, with a highly amused doorkeeper at the hotel.

'He called me a swaggering brat and a slinker round the homes of honest men and said that I should be in purdah,' Roberta said defensively, 'so

I said he was less than the dung of a three-legged jackal and would poison the vultures when he died.'

Jessica wondered briefly what had happened to the quiet little girl who had lived in London. 'I don't think that was terribly polite, darling,' Jessica said gently, 'and not the sort of thing you should say in England.'

'But this is India, Mummy,' Roberta said in English, 'and,' she continued in Urdu, 'nobody insults a Pathan and Pathan women are proud and not harem chattels. Zaheena told me that,' she went on virtuously, 'and Wazir Khan and Zaheena say that I am Pathan when dressed as a Pathan and Missy memsahib when I'm not. It's quite simple,' she finished patiently.

'It's been a wonderful honeymoon, darling,' Jessica said to Guy as she lay beside him in bed, relaxed, happy. 'I can't believe that I could be so happy.'

Guy stretched lazily, his arm moving to hug her to him. 'It's not over yet, my love,' he answered, 'the best is yet to come, at least in terms of travel,' he amended hastily. 'We'll be at Dharmsala the day after tomorrow.' He yawned. 'Best dress for you,' he said, 'you'll be handing over the cheque and making a speech.' His voice was suddenly drowsy. 'Be good for your Urdu,' he mumbled.

Jessica lay awake as Guy drifted away into a deep sleep. She loved him dearly and her life had changed so radically in the last months. She smiled again at the memory of Roberta, fiercely defending her adopted race. That same evening, she recalled, Roberta had been clean and scrubbed in a blue frock and had behaved impeccably throughout the evening as a well brought up English child. Her daughter was rapidly becoming absurdly mature, well-adjusted, all the things that Jessica wanted her to be, and it had all happened because of Guy. She put her arm round him and soon she, too, was asleep.

The orphanage was a hotch-potch

of buildings, grey stone, red brick, a bewildering variety of style. It had been a long journey to reach it, flying to the nearest airstrip in a tiny aircraft into which they had all crammed and then by battered Land Rover, the road becoming steadily worse until it finally degenerated into a rutted track. The mass of the Himalayas shone in the distance and the Land Rover wheezed and coughed as it climbed into the foothills.

Jessica stretched gratefully when she finally was able to get out of the vehicle as it stopped in the cobbled courtyard and looked around her. She was immediately surrounded by hordes of smiling children. Guy fought his way to her side.

'This is it,' he said simply.

'Mr Tankerton, sir! You are finally arriving!'

Jessica stared at the beaming figure, in European clothes, who was shouting from the cool darkness of the orphanage. His skin was dark, obviously Indian, the grey was thick in his hair, his English accented but rapid and fluent.

'John Stanhope,' Guy muttered, 'English blood from way back. He's the administrator.' Guy raised a hand in cheerful greeting. 'Come on,' he urged, 'this is the social bit.'

'I am very pleased to be meeting you again, Mr Tankerton,' John Stanhope said enthusiastically, 'and this is the charming bride of whom you were writing to me.' His teeth were very white when he smiled. He held out his hand. 'I am much pleased to be making your acquaintance.,'

'I've spent the last months looking forward to this moment very much,' Jessica answered sincerely.

'First we will be having tea,' Stanhope said, 'and then you will be wishing to clean up after your jolly hard journey. I dare say your fine Pathan will be finding the bungalow without fuss.'

'He seemed to be heading in that direction the last I saw,' Guy said easily.

'Everything there is jolly fine,' said Stanhope, 'it is still used often. Many times we are getting Army patrols visiting because of all the damned troubles and the officer stays there.' He beamed again. 'Now let us be having a cup of good tea and we can be discussing the ceremony for handing over the cheque. Tomorrow, I have arranged for it and a photographer also to record the happy occasion. My goodness,' he said, 'one million pounds, we will be building fine new buildings and getting more beds for the hospital.'

'My wife will make the actual presentation,' Guy said casually, as they drank their tea. 'I thought it appropriate that another Jessica Tankerton should do it.'

John Stanhope put down his cup with a clatter and stared at Jessica. 'Am I hearing properly,' he said curiously, 'your name is Jessica?' He turned to Guy. 'You were not giving your lovely wife's name when you are writing to me,' he said, a faint shade of indignation in his words.

Jessica smiled at him. 'Yes. It's a happy coincidence.'

John Stanhope's eyes were very still, ripe damsons full of thought. 'There is no such thing as coincidence, Mrs Tankerton,' he said simply. 'Some things are ordained.' He picked up his cup. 'After you are handing over the money,' he said, 'perhaps you would be seeing round the orphanage?' The suggestion was curiously firm.

'I'd like that,' Jessica agreed quickly. It was something she wanted to do. 'And I'd like you to tell me the history of the place. It looks utterly fascinating.'

'I'll miss out on that,' Guy put in hastily, 'we're here for a couple of weeks so I shall have plenty of time to renew old acquaintances.' He gave an easy smile. 'Wazir Khan and I might take ourselves up into the hills for the day,' he said.

John Stanhope nodded. 'It will be

my privilege to be looking after Mrs Tankerton,' he said eagerly, 'and talking much of times past here.'

Jessica blinked as the flashgun exploded. John Stanhope waved the cheque and Roberta and Guy gazed solemnly at the camera as another photograph was taken. There was a burst of clapping and the children started to sing. Jessica stood patiently until the song finished and clapped in her turn.

'Right,' said Guy quickly, 'I'll leave you to the tour of inspection, darling. I'm off to change and I'll see you for dinner.' He leaned forward and kissed her lightly on the cheek. 'I'll hand Roberta over to Zaheena,' he said, 'they're cooking up something, I'm sure.'

Roberta looked at him scornfully. 'We're making Teddy a suit,' she said, 'a Pathan one. Zaheena is teaching me to sew.'

Jessica waved as they walked away and turned to the administrator.

John Stanhope coughed discreetly. 'Perhaps you are wanting to see everything?' he asked.

Jessica nodded. 'Absolutely everything,' she confirmed.

'First then, we are going in museum,' John Stanhope said, 'only one room, but shows the history here. Picture of Miss Jessica who founded this place and of my ancestor who was first administrator. Passed from father to son, you know, he was fine army officer, formed Stanhope's Frontier Horse to put down rebels, very class regiment, Pathan, Sikh, Mahratta squadrons,' he explained cheerfully, hardly pausing for breath. 'He became general for a prince, very distinguished man, and then left to run the orphanage because Miss Jessica asked him.' He smiled proudly. 'Fine ancestor to have, William Stanhope.'

'William Stanhope!' Excitement raced through Jessica's voice.

'You are already hearing of William, I think,' the administrator said carefully, 'Mr Tankerton told me you were

254

writing life of Miss Jessica.' He opened a door. 'In here please, Mrs Jessica Tankerton,' he invited politely.

So this was William at last, Jessica thought as she studied the faded sepia photograph on the wall which hung next to one of a determined Jessica. No wonder the old lady had fallen for him. He was tall, and his face was stern and proud, keen-featured with a heavy, curling moustache and long sideburns. The photograph had been taken when he was still an army officer for he stood proudly in a uniform which dripped lace decoration.

'When did he die?'

'He lived a very long time,' Stanhope said, 'more than ninety years. 1926 he was buried. My father was knowing him very well. Of course,' John Stanhope said, 'he was leaving English service to be free lance with Indian prince because his mother was Indian.' He cleared his throat. 'Damn problem at time, English father, Indian mother, after rebels were put down.'

'I see,' Jessica said carefully. It was obviously a delicate matter.

'Mrs Jessica Tankerton, please.'

She turned to see John Stanhope staring at her with a curious look on his face.

He went to a safe in the corner and opened it. 'My father is giving me this trust,' he said, 'and he is getting it direct from William.' He reached inside and pulled out a large tin deed box. 'Before he died, William gave this box to my father and told him to keep it sealed and only ever hand it over to Jessica Tankerton. My father is thinking that William is mad man but it was a solemn instruction, so he obeyed. William insisted Jessica Tankerton would come again one day and would need the box.' His dark eyes were still. 'My father gave me also this trust,' he said, 'and I would pass it to my son in turn.' He reached inside his shirt, pulled out a necklace of string from which hung a key. 'Always, I am keeping this safe,' he said. 'Now, I am thinking that the trust is discharged because Jessica Tankerton has come back.'

Jessica started at him. 'How very curious,' she said.

The Indian bobbed his head, suddenly embarrassed. 'William was right,' he said simply, 'Jessica Tankerton returned.' He smiled. 'You are knowing he lived in the bungalow?'

'He did?' Jessica gaped at the administrator.

'Yes, indeed. It was first home for administrator, being built even before the orphanage. Miss Jessica stayed there when she visited.' The smile came again. 'You and Mr Tankerton are staying in William's very own bedroom.' He gave a tiny giggle, 'the very same one,' he repeated. 'Now please,' he said, 'be looking at picture of orphanage in 1900 when visited by local dignitaries. Very interesting, I think.'

'I didn't even know that there was a box,' Guy said that evening. He looked at it. 'Have you opened it?' he asked.

'I waited for you,' Jessica answered. 'It's something we both ought to share.' She frowned. 'In fact, it's yours, not mine. I'm only a Tankerton by marriage.'

'Don't talk nonsense, darling,' Guy said. 'You're my wife and that makes you a fully paid up member of the Tankerton clan. Come on, open up.'

Jessica turned the key in the lock. It turned as easily as if it were brand-new. She lifted the lid. The box was full of papers and some small books and Jessica knew she had found the missing diaries. She picked up the first few, removed a layer of paper and gasped. Glinting up at her, gold and blood red, were the earrings in Jessica Tankerton's portrait!

12

'If Sahib Guy wants his bath before the lecky light finishes,' Wazir Khan said firmly, 'then he must hurry. Also, memsahib, your bath too is waiting.'

Jessica put back the papers in the box, covering the earrings, and locked it. 'I'm sure that there's a full explanation, darling,' she said, 'and I'll look through the papers sometime.'

'The old girl must have sent them out to raise money, I suppose,' Guy hazarded, 'and somehow they got overlooked.'

'You're probably right,' Jessica said, 'now go and have your bath before you seize up after all your walking today.' Guy did not know that William had been the old lady's lover. Jessica had not told him what she had learnt from the diaries. Her fingers itched to sort through the papers, read what was there, unravel the secret. There had to be a reason why Jessica had sent the earrings to William.

'If the sahib and memsahib would care to imitate the action of the monkey meeting a tiger,' Wazir Khan broke in politely, 'lamps can be lit and fires started while they bathe. Missy memsahib is already bathed and ready for bed,' he concluded.

Jessica sat in the bath listening to the steady chug of the generator which provided electricity to the compound. It worked only for a few hours each evening to save fuel and was switched off once all the children were in bed. There was no mains water or central heating in the bungalow but open fireplaces or cast-iron stoves in every room. A huge communal logpile provided the fuel for the domestic quarters. Jessica had hardly noticed her surroundings the previous night because she had been so tired. She and Guy had tumbled into bed and fallen asleep while the generator was still working.

It was only now that she began to realise that nothing had changed very much since Jessica Tankerton had first founded the orphanage.

She got out of the bath at the very moment that the generator's steady heartbeat stopped. The lights flickered and faded, leaving her in darkness. There was a gentle tap at the door and Zaheena entered gracefully, carrying an oil lamp, its flickering flame sending huge hadows across the bathroom.

Jessica wrapped herself in a towel and smiled thanks at the Pathan girl. They had become friends in the few weeks since they had first met and Jessica had begun to understand the relationship between Guy and Wazir Khan because she and Zaheena were moving towards a similar one. It was unlike anything she had ever known, Jessica thought as she dried between her toes, because Zaheena was not a conventional servant and nor was Wazir Khan. They chose to serve with pride and there was an equality, curious — even bizarre — to conventional European thought, in the relationship. It was love, Jessica decided slowly, a love which grew like any other from respect and understanding, mutual loyalty and acceptance.

'Would it be possible,' Jessica asked John Stanhope the next morning, 'to have a copy of the photograph of William? I'd like it for my book.'

'I am arranging it with all expediency,' John Stanhope said, 'very easy to do. I will be instructing the photographwala and be making sure it is jolly well done. He will be delivering pictures of yesterday's great occasion later so I will be asking him then.' He chortled happily. 'It is very great pleasure to be helping in this way.'

Jessica smiled at him. 'I'd like to learn more about William,' she said, 'because I think he played quite a big part in Jessica Tankerton's life.'

John Stanhope bobbed his head. 'Very much known in the family,' he said, 'and my own father wrote it all down. I will give you a copy,' he offered, 'so you can be reading it back in England and thinking of us here.'

'Thank you.' Jessica paused. 'William's box was full of papers,' she said casually, 'and I think I will have to take them back to England as well. I won't have the time to go through them here. Do you mind?'

'Why should I?' Stanhope sounded puzzled. 'They were to be handed to Jessica Tankerton and that I have done. I am being confident that you will do what is necessary.' His voice acquired a curious inflection. 'Nothing happens by chance, my dear Jessica Tankerton,' he said, 'and karma may take a hundred years to show itself.' He giggled, his tone normal again. 'I am being told by my father that William used to say that when he was very old and he was very mystic and strange in his ways.' He gave a smile. 'It does not mean anything, I am thinking.'

Guy took Jessica and Roberta out riding in the hills the next two days. It was a great adventure because they would be camping overnight. Wazir Khan and Zaheena went with them, happy to be in the mountains. It was surprisingly cold, Jessica found, and she was grateful for the Pathan-style animal skin coat and clothing that Zaheena produced for her. Roberta was wrapped up as well and Guy, blond hair hidden by a turban, could have been a Pathan himself. During the weeks they had been in India, their exposed skin had tanned. Jessica caught a glimpse of herself in the mirror before they left and realised with a start that, dressed as she was, she could have easily passed as a woman from one of the hill tribes and Roberta was indistinguishable from many of the children at the orphanage when she was in her local clothing. Jessica grinned to herself. If ever Roberta had to write an essay on what she had done in the holidays, it would read like an adventure story.

They spent the night in a cave. Jessica snuggled up close to Guy as they all sat round a blazing fire. Wazir Khan and Zaheena had conjured up a glorious meal which bubbled away in a communal pot and they had all dipped bowls into it, scorning knives and forks and eating happily. It was a marvellous way to spend a honeymoon, Jessica thought, as she wandered back into the darkness at the rear of the cave where Wazir Khan had spread out the bedding rolls for Guy and herself. Roberta had her own space, equidistant between her and the Pathans who would be sleeping much closer to the fire.

The flames threw great black shadows and jumping patches of light onto the walls. Jessica stopped and shook her head in disbelief as a log dropped and flared up sending a sudden shaft of light that lit up the back of the cave.

She knelt, hands trembling, and stared at the letters cut into the wall. The flame died away and her fingers were left to trace them in the sudden darkness.

WSJTAUG1871

Jessica shivered at the tremor that bolted through her body. William Stanhope Jessica Tankerton August 1871. That had to be it. The first Jessica had been in this very cave with William so many years before. It was the only possible interpretation and Jessica suddenly felt a pagan, wanton impulse running through her body that she could not deny.

Guy came to her that night in the cool darkness of the cave with a tenderness and consideration that was even more finely tuned than ever. Her fingers held to him desperately as the growing wave of love inside her grew bigger, ever bigger, before crashing in an exultant roar of triumph and she felt Guy's gift of life enter her, knew that their love was to be crowned, thankful that she would nurture their child inside her and she clung to him, her heart rejoicing as the slow return from that ultimate pleasure gradually slowed her reeling senses and she heard his sweet, murmured phrases of love in her ear.

The photograph of William Stanhope, together with copies of the pictures that had been taken when she handed over the cheque, were waiting for her when they returned from the hills.

Guy peered over her shoulder as she looked at William's picture. 'Smart looking devil, William Stanhope,' he said casually. His hand whispered along the nape of her neck. 'Ruled this place with a rod of iron apparently. Old Jessica refused to retire him and he soldiered on for years. He didn't give up the job until after the First World War and then his son took over and so on up to the present day.' Guy smiled. 'It's as good a way to run the place as any.'

Jessica looked at the photograph again. The copy was blacker, less faded than the original. William had certainly been handsome. The face was hard yet Jessica could imagine how it could become tender, loving. A shiver ran through her as she stared at it, a familiarity about it nagged at her.

'You appear quite the grand lady,' Guy observed lightly, flipping over the other photographs, 'and Roberta looks remarkably respectable. Certainly one for the old family album,' he said and stretched. 'I am going to get in my bath,' he said. 'Tomorrow is hard work day. I'll be discussing everything with John and we'll be making some decisions.' He hugged her. 'Do you want to get involved directly, or let me tell you about it later?' he asked.

Jessica made up her mind. 'I'd like to look through the box of papers,' she said slowly, 'I had intended to wait until we got back to England but I want to do it earlier.' She turned to Guy. 'Darling,' she said, 'I know exactly why this place is so important to you. We will be coming back, won't we?'

Guy kissed her. 'As often as you wish,' he said, and his eyes were bright, 'I'm just so happy that both you and Roberta are as enchanted as I am with it all.' His embrace tightened. 'I love you so much.' There was a tiny silence. 'One thing,' he said, 'dig the earrings out of the box for me, would you?'

Dismay swamped Jessica. 'You're not going to sell them, are you?' she asked.

'Why not? That's probably why she sent them here.'

'They were in the portrait,' Jessica stammered, 'they meant a lot to her.' She drew a deep breath. 'Anyway, we don't know and I might find out.' She was aware that Guy was chuckling, the blue eyes dancing with love and laughter.

'Darling heart,' he said, 'selling them is the thing furthest from my mind. I promise you will have them back inside three days. In fact,' he said, 'if it sets your mind at rest, one of them will suffice perfectly well.'

Jessica frowned at him. 'What are you up to?' she demanded suspiciously.

Guy put a finger of his lips. 'I am like the three wise monkeys,' he joked, 'and you will find out all in good time.

With that, you have to be patient.'

She would find the diary for 1871, Jessica decided when she was finally able to sit down the next day and look at the contents of the box. She had given one of the earrings to Guy the previous evening and he had merely looked pleased in an annoying way. He was up to something.

She looked quickly through the diaries, quick eyes looking for dates and gave a swift sigh of satisfaction when she found the right one. She turned the pages carefully and found the entry for which she was looking:

'*Aug 20th 1871* Wm took me up into the Hills two Days ago and We Have just Return'd. He Made me wear Native Dress for altho' the Land is Settled Under a Beneficent Rule, there are still Bandits and Others who Might Capture and Hold a Memsahib for Ransom. Wm Also was Dressed as a Native & a Casual Observer would Not have Dreamed that We were Europeans. We Camped And I

Asked Him what I could Do to Help this Land Which Has Taught Me So Much. I Have Seen So Many Beggars in the Cities and Indeed Elsewhere that it Seems only Right That I should try to Provide Some Relief. Wm Gave His Opinion that an Orphanage Should Be Founded. He Told Me how Many of his Soldiers Left Widows and Orphans if They Were Killed In this Inhospitable Terrain and That Public Relief was Often Most Inadequate. Underneath his Martial Ardour And Bearing, he is the Kindest Of Souls, Gentle and Caring. When I First Met Him I Thought Him Just Another Soldier, like Dearest Papa With Little Thought for Aught But Campaigning and Cantonments. How Wrong I was! And I Have Never Regretted Offering Myself to him For he has brought Such Joy, such Pleasure to Me, Delights that I never Dreamed of!'

So the orphanage was William's idea! Guy would be interested to learn that in due course. She pondered over the entry for a moment before reading on.

'We Camped Overnight in a Cave which Wm had Stumbled Upon Earlier During His Travels In The Hills. We Sat And Talked about His Plan. Now That the Country is Settled, the Orphanage could Be Located in One of the Old Forts Which are Scattered About This Area. Conversion Would Not Be Expensive, Barrack Rooms etc Being Easily Made Into Children's Dormitories and Wm Said If I Did do Such a Thing, He Would Leave the Service and Run It. An Orphan He Said Was As Much Entitled to Justice and a Chance To Make Good As any other. I Was Much Moved By His Sentiments And When We Retired, I was More Than Anxious For The Act of Love Which He Brought To Me.'

Jessica felt her cheeks flush. Two Jessicas with but a single thought, she said to herself. She continued reading and suddenly her attention was riveted on another entry. She hardly noticed when Zaheena padded into the room with coffee, but continued to read, slowly beginning to understand and appreciate what her predecessor had done.

Jessica closed the diary, lost in thought, and put it away carefully in the tin box. The photographs were still on the table and she picked up the picture of William Stanhope again and studied it in detail. She thought she knew why the face was familiar. She felt in her handbag, found a pen and turned to the photograph of herself with Guy and Roberta. She took a deep breath, and with William's photograph in front of her, carefully sketched in his moustache and sideburns on Guy's smiling expression.

She was right! When she had finished, she was looking at the face of William Stanhope!

She drank the cold coffee and started to read the rest of the diary. It all slotted into place. The first Jessica Tankerton had been one determined lady. She picked up the other diaries.

Jessica had visited India regularly and these were the records of each trip. She had brought Camilla out with her when the child was about six or seven years old, the same age as Roberta Jessica realised with a shock, and they had stayed in this same bungalow, the bungalow which was occupied by the administrator of the orphanage, William Stanhope and Camilla's father!

It was late afternoon when Jessica finished reading and she had pieced together the full story. She felt a glow of success. The first Jessica had become pregnant, the result of the encounter in the cave and she wasn't the only one, Jessica was swiftly, certainly sure of that. It was social disaster. William was Anglo-Indian, a cardinal sin in Victorian England. Jessica Tankerton had written about it quite calmly in her diary, accepting her fate without complaint and, without warning, there had been a lifeline. Cholera. Her Cousin Rodney and his wife had died of it. Jessica had merely adapted the tragedy to her own use, claiming simply that the child was theirs. In fact, Jessica had not travelled upcountry to rescue her cousin's baby. There wasn't one. It was Camilla, Jessica's own child, born discreetly in a hospital run by Catholic nuns and well away from any European settlement, with William passing himself off as her legitimate husband. As soon as possible after the birth, Jessica had travelled back to England to add as much gloss to the story of rescuing the cousin's baby as she could. Jessica suddenly realised why the diary entry she had read in England had been incongruous. It was the mention of baptism. The baby would have been baptised as soon as possible after the birth. Death in tropical countries was no stranger to infants. In fact, she considered wryly, little Camilla might even have been baptised a Catholic and old Jessica Tankerton was covering up again!

The letters that had passed over the years between William and Jessica were in the box together with the final letter of all:

'*18th May 1917* My Most Dear William. The Strain of This Dreadful War and The Accumulation Of Years Makes Me Sure That We Shall Not Meet Again in This Life. I Cling, Dearest Love, To the Belief That We Shall Be Reunited Either in the Next World or as Reincarnated Souls In This. It is a Philosophy Which, I Doubt, Would Appeal to More Conventional Minds. I Am Sending You Every Letter That You Sent Me as well as My Diaries Which Tell Our Story. Keep Them, My Love, until I Come For Them Again. Also, My Heart, My Prince, I Send The Earrings,the Earrings You Gave Me the Day you Learned That I had Conceived the Living Symbol of Our Love. One Day, Perhaps, The Story Of What Happened Between Us Can Be Told. Until That Day, I Fear It must remain Hidden. Camilla Will Never Know. The World Would Not

Understand But I Have Kept Faith My Love As I Know You Would Wish. I Do Believe That We Will Meet Again and That Our Love Will Be Fulfilled Openly. Only You and I Know That there Will Be Part of You and Me in Every Tankerton. My Only Regret Is That You Never Were Able To Come Here To England. It Is So Lovely in the Spring and From My Bedroom To Which I Am Now Largely Confined I can See The Hills That Remind Me Daily of the Place Where Our Child Was Conceived. You Would Not, I Fear My Love Recognise the Old Woman Who Writes these Words as the Girl Who Came To You So Long Ago and Made Obeisance and Murmured Mai Aapsar Pyar Karthihu. Farewell My Heart. Your Devoted Jessica'

13

'Bhai-bund Daddy,' Roberta asked thoughtfully, 'we will be coming back to India again, won't we?' She tugged at Guy's hand. 'Teddy wants to,' she announced.

Guy swung her up in the air and she gave a delighted squeal. 'Not if we have to take back as much as we have accumulated on this trip,' he growled and hugged her to him. 'All we need is a stuffed tiger and we'll have everything.' He swung her round in a circle. 'Of course, of course,' he said happily, 'as many times as you want to.' He put her back on the ground.

Guy looked at his watch and turned to Jessica. 'We're in good time,' he said. 'We should be in Delhi tonight.'

'All of the packing is finished,' Jessica confirmed. William Stanhope's precious tin box had been stowed firmly away in one of Jessica's cases. 'We'll spend years getting through Customs with it all,' she finished mournfully.

Guy smiled. 'Everything is written down,' he said, 'unless you've sneaked a few things in that I don't know about. I shall present the list with charm and courtesy and be resigned to whatever may befall. His face straightened. 'Come on,' he said, 'time to make our farewells.'

Jessica smiled back at him and looked out towards the distant peaks of the Himalayas, etched against the blue sky. A faint plume of white was blowing across the mountains, snow whipped up by the wind. The air was so clear that it could be seen from miles away. Justin had died out there, his body lost, still there, deep under the snows. 'Yes, my love,' she said softly, 'time to make our farewells.'

Tankerton Hall was grey, disappearing into a pewter sky, as they reached home again. Roberta bounced up and down excitedly as the car turned along the drive and pulled up in front of the main door.

Four smiling Tibetans bobbed up and down, tongues poking out, as they rushed to help unload the cases. Wazir Khan swaggered proudly around, presenting Zaheena to them. They were home again.

Guy took Jessica's hand. 'Come to the library,' he said, 'there's something I want to give you.'

Jessica followed him, puzzled.

Guy stood her in front of the portrait of old Jessica Tankerton and Camilla. He cleared his throat. 'Do you remember,' he began, 'that not so long ago, I asked you to marry me?'

Jessica gaped at him. 'You idiot,' she replied, 'how could I not? And, in case you have forgotten, I agreed and we did. Get married, that is.'

Guy gave an exasperated groan. 'Let me finish,' he said, 'I've been working up to this for the past fortnight. Don't spoil my big moment.' He grinned. 'I'll start again.'

Jessica shook her head. 'You're crazy.'

'One of the conventional things,' Guy said relentlessly, 'is to get engaged and then married and signify the engagement by the presentation of a ring. Don't say anything,' he warned as Jessica opened her mouth. He felt in his pocket. 'It was something I overlooked,' he said, 'but now I've made it right. This is for you, Jessica Tankerton.' He pulled a small box out of his pocket.

'Darling!' Jessica said, catching her breath in amazement as she peeped inside, 'it's perfect. It matches exactly!' The ring was gold with a single gleaming ruby, the design following the same filigree work as on the earrings. 'Now I know,' she said, 'why you were so mysterious with the Customs officer and sent me away.'

She flung her arms about his neck and kissed him. 'Darling Guy,' she said, 'I love you with all my heart!' She thrust the box at him. 'Put it on my finger then, you unromantic,

wonderful, gorgeous, light of my life!'
He didn't realise how appropriate,
how magnificently right it was, Jessica
thought.

Guy slipped the ring onto her finger.

'I think I have some news for you
as well,' Jessica said carefully. 'It's very
early, but I know.'

Guy's eyebrows lifted in a silent
question.

'It's about Zaheena,' Jessica said
precisely, 'and what she is going to
do in this household.' She fought to
keep her face straight.

Guy looked bewildered. 'Help Wazir
Khan and the things she does for you,'
he suggested helplessly.

'Actually,' Jessica said, 'I think she
might have her hands full in about
eight months from now. I shall need
an ayah, my prince.'

'A nursemaid?' Guy said, puzzled,
and then his face became radiant. 'Are
you sure?'

Jessica nodded. 'The cave,' she said
simply.

Guy put his arms round her in a gigantic hug. 'We'll have to think of names,' he said excitedly. 'There are traditional ones in the family, you know.'

Jessica disengaged herself with the gentlest of movements. 'It has already been decided,' she murmured softly, 'a karma must be fulfilled. A girl will be called Camilla, a boy William.'

'William?' Guy's voice was all question.

Jessica kissed him. 'It's a long story, darling,' she said softly, 'all about Camilla and your great great grand-father and the first Jessica.' She laughed at the look on his face. 'My love, my own love,' she whispered huskily, 'I shall tell you all about it before the baby is born!'

Other titles in the
Linford Romance Library:

VOYAGE INTO PERIL

Shirley Allen

Julia had spent the past three years in America with her mother and stepfather, George. After the death of her mother, Julia decided to return with George to the Isle of Man, where she had been born and brought up. As they sailed from New York on board the Lusitania, she met again the man who had stolen her heart years before. But danger lurked in the seas. Was the love she longed for to elude her yet again?

THE FLAUNTING MOON

Catherine Darby

Purity Makin is only a girl when James Rodale, a handsome cavalier, seeks shelter at Ladymoon Manor, the house on the moors which holds strange echoes of its sinister past. But the girl has the passions of a woman, and from the events of a night springs a tale of promises betrayed and twisted jealousies; a tale in which a sacred chalice is used for good or evil to satisfy the desires of those who discover the secret of the Moon Goddess.

A MAN FOR ALWAYS

Nancy John

After the plane crash that robbed her of her memory, they told her that her name was Jayne Stewart, and she could only accept and tremble. She trembled with humiliation, for Jayne was cold and calculating, a woman who hadn't cared when her husband died. And she trembled with passion, passion for her husband's brother, Duncan, a man who had sworn to hate her. What was the truth about her past? Would she find it in time to bring her love in the present — and for always?

DANGEROUS LOVE

Caroline Joyce

Rebellion had brought many hardships to her beloved country and Rosaleen feared for the safety of her father and brothers when they became involved in the 1798 County Wexford rebellion. When she meets Captain Geraint Glendower, the brother-in-law of the farmer for whom she works, Rosaleen finds herself becoming very attracted to him. But the last thing she needs in these troubled times is to become torn between her family and her love for a British army officer.

SHADOWS OF THE PAST

Margaret McDonagh

To take her mind off her Great Aunt Rosemary's pending operation, Holly decided to visit Pagham Harbour Nature Reserve. When she became stuck in the mudflats, handsome Rick Cunningham came to her rescue. Holly found herself becoming attracted to Rick, who was a partner in a firm of architects in Chichester. But when he told her of his plans for Rosemary's cottage, she was shattered. How could she ever trust him again?

PENDRAGON:
THE WIZARD'S DAUGHTER

Katrina Wright

In the winter of 1594, Nimue, daughter of the Queen's 'other Welsh wizard', has left London for North Wales to find her destiny. The playwright Will Shakespeare follows her as his Dark Lady, but she has met Merlin Pendragon, the scarred lord of Pendragon tower, and feels they have shared a passionate bond in the past. Against the background of land-greed and fever for the newly-discovered Welsh gold, Nimue and Pendragon are married. But before she can go to him, events overtake them . . .